Birthright

Cadillac Press

Cadillac Press
185 Drummond St. Rd
Drummond, NB E3Y 1V9
Canada

Cover image by Taria Reed

2 4 6 8 10 9 7 5 3 1
FIRST EDITION THIS PUBLISHER

This book is dedicated to my editors, my critique partners, and to Barb and Katja, my beta readers. Without you, this book would not be a reality. You're all awesome!

Birthright

Wendy L. Koenig

Chapter 1

Fiera watched the body of her mother slowly disappear. One-by-one, the villagers placed their stones on the woman that had borne her and, until that morning, had brushed her hair every day. Her father lay nearby, under his own pile, settled from rains that had come too late for her parents. Now Fiera was alone. With her parents' death just days from each other, it was as if she had died, too.

She bore her grief in every pore of her body. Yet, she stood by and did nothing. Leery villagers filed past, offering condolences. The neighbor woman, who sometimes entertained soldiers, took her gingerly by the waist and guided her home to a table filled with meager offerings of food.

The bereaved eagerly ate and mostly left her alone, sneaking quick looks when they thought she didn't see, then turning back to their friends, shaking their heads sadly.

For hours this lasted, and would have gone all night, but Fiera rose to her feet, stumbled out the door, and back to the graves of her family. The sun had given way to night and it had started raining again. A fine shower hugged her as she lowered herself to huddle between her parents. The water slipped into the ground and disappeared, leaving the soil as hard and cracked as before, not enough to erase the hunger of either the land or its people. Tomorrow, there would still be dust.

The neighbor woman followed with a lard-thickened blanket that was meant to lie beneath a traveler as they slept in the open night. She drew it tightly around Fiera and left, muttering, "We'll probably be at her funeral within a few days' time."

Nineteen and Fiera was alone. If she'd married like others much younger, then she'd have had a husband and his family to help her through. Then again, they might have died from the famine as well.

Slowly, the understanding of her sudden freedom crept over her. Rising, and with no plans or sense of her direction, she stumbled across the broken land in the rain, her blanket as her only shelter. Through the night she walked on hunger weakened muscles, at times falling to lie in a crumpled heap until the awful ache within her heart drove her on. The rain ceased, leaving the ground dry and choking, as if water had never touched it. At long last, she came to a road and the struggle of whether to turn east or west sapped the remains of her energy. She slumped to the ground, waiting for fate to decide her death.

Finally, in the dawn hour, Fiera heard the *clack* of hooves on stone, the creak of braces, and the low toneless hum of a merchant coming from the east.

She struggled to her feet and tugged the blanket to cover her tangled fawn-red hair. The effort to hide herself had a cost and she tipped toward the ground. In what she supposed could be considered a miracle, she managed to stay on her feet by flailing her arms and stumbling a few steps.

A giant single-horse cart appeared from around a bend. It was loaded with rattling pots and pans, bolts of fabric, herbs, jars of assorted nails, and other items. A huge dappled grey horse slowly pulled at the traces while an ancient man with a long white drooping moustache hunched on a seat with thick springs and an even thicker pad.

"Whoa!" The aged merchant heavily leaned back on the reins, sawing at the horse's mouth. He peered at her in the awakening light. "What do we have here?"

Too weary to speak, Fiera waited for the merchant to decide what to do about her, swaying on her feet like a leaf on one of the dying trees around her.

After a long slow consideration, the old man pursed his lips. "Well, come on, then. You can climb up by yourself, can't you?"

Dumbly, she shuffled toward the cart. The giant draft horse looked her in the eye, its thoughts in her head. *Witch, beware of this man. He steals from other merchants and the poor. He only feeds me when he steals.*

Fiera paused at the horse's muscled neck, giving it long strokes, in part to buy time while she spoke with the horse, but also to steady herself. Animals always knew the truth. She wasn't surprised this one had seen her identity, but horses rarely cared about the affairs of men until it affected them, such as this horse's hunger. She would be wise to consider its words. If the animal was to be believed, the merchant wasn't to be trusted.

11

Will you carry me?

The horse bobbed its head. *Anywhere.*

With shaking fingers, she smoothed her hands over the brace buckles, feeling them disappear beneath her fingers. *You will need to lower yourself so I can mount.*

"What's going on?" The old man rose from his seat, the springs squawking from lack of grease, and he peered down at her. "Stop! What are you doing?"

He tied off the reins. As he climbed down from the cart, the braces dropped to the ground and the horse lowered to its knees. Fiera slid across its wide back and wound one hand through its thick mane, her other hand tightly clutching the blanket around her. She clamped her legs around the horse's ribs. Even still, the horse nearly unseated her as it lunged to its feet and they took off, two steps ahead of the cursing merchant. She only hoped she had enough strength to stay mounted for the journey.

Hunkered low over the horse's muscled shoulders, they flew past thinly foliaged trees and brush that was nothing more than sticks, leaves long dried and blown away. Watching the landscape blow past dizzied her, so she concentrated on the road instead. The horse's hooves burst the dust off the ground like small explosions. Boom-boom...boom. Boom-boom...boom.

She asked, *What's your name?*

I'm called Captain. I was first a soldier's horse.

I'm Fiera.

Fire! Like your hair?

Yes. Like my hair. The brown of bare trees ripped past as the clouds above dissipated. Beneath her, the boom-boom...boom took her further away from her only home. She turned and looked behind them at the dust trail that became a wall between her and the past. There would be no more hiding, no more shame. Despite the ache in her heart over the loss of her parents, she smiled. It was time for a new beginning.

Her traveling companion seemed to enjoy the journey. He stretched his long neck forward and tossed his head. *Where are we going?*

Anywhere there was life. Her heart hurt for her parents, yes, but it also ached for the friendship of her own kind: witches. And it ached for something else, something she couldn't quite define. *As far away as we can.*

****

Efar stood on the doorstep of the little cottage that had been his home for the last four months. He reached up and placed his hands inside the doorway, not so much as to stretch, but more to keep himself in place. The beast within him surged, reminding him that he was not one person, but sometimes two. His fingers beat a staccato rhythm on the ancient wood as he let his gaze rove the valley.

Lush green trees, thick grass, and flowers of nearly every hue and fragrance were interspersed with bold swaths of golden grain and vegetable plants heavy with produce. The pigs were fat, cows and goats swung pendulous udders, and the horses frolicked in the field.

Behind him, in the cabin, worked a beautiful woman, Gabriella, with long black hair, honey-colored skin, full lips, and patience in her eyes. The exact opposite of him. He was fair-skinned, blond, blue-eyed, and impatient with most things, but trying to learn to be different.

He had a reputation as being fond of the ladies. Of never being able to settle down. His mother, out of desperation, had turned to her brother, the King of the Griffins, who had set him up to run this small holding.

13

Gabriella was the wife of a fallen soldier. Not of his choosing. Yet, he'd been quite taken by her when they'd met.

He had everything any man could want. So, why was he thinking of leaving?

His fingers stopped drumming. He knew the reason: he wasn't in love. He and Gabriella had tried to be. It just wasn't working. And she, with the long-enduring patience of a saint, would never tell him to leave. Though he knew she wanted him to go.

He barked a laugh and shook his head. Such was the story of his life. Why couldn't he be like most men: stay, work the farm, raise babies, love or not? Gabriella would keep him comfortable.

He dropped his arms. Because, he wanted more than comfort. He wanted passion. Somewhere, a woman with fire in her eyes and bravery in her heart waited for him. His woman. He couldn't rest until he found her.

He turned back toward the dim light of the cottage, but he couldn't make himself step all the way inside. He raised his gaze and met Gabriella's patient eyes. She knew he had to find his own way. Be his own man.

Without saying a word, he pivoted and walked into the bank of trees. He wasn't going to worry about her. She wouldn't be working the farm alone for very long. During the time he'd been with her, he'd chased off three would-be lovers. It wouldn't take her long to find a new "husband", probably someone more suited to her. She'd be fine.

As soon as he was out of sight, he undressed and loosed the creature within him. It grew and stretched, his bones aching with each inch they lengthened. He could change in the blink of an eye, but there was a price to pay if he did. The pain would be excruciating, nearly blinding.

So, he kept it slow, taking long minutes to become the creature. His arms thickened heavily until they touched the ground with fingers that sharpened into talons. His back broadened and wings sprouted on his shoulder blades, spreading to a span of nearly fifteen feet. A fine coating of golden brown fur coated his skin from his feet until just below his wings where it changed to feathers that covered all the rest of his upper body, including his face. His already large nose increased, becoming an eagle's beak and his hips and legs changed to that of a giant cat's, complete with lion's tail.

When he finished shifting, he stood a little over nine feet tall, small for a griffin. He clacked his beak. He may be small, but he was fast. More than once he'd taught his taunting brethren to respect that. There were no other creatures in the sky that could catch him.

Efar launched into the air, thrusting hard with all the strength of his wings. The giddiness of freedom filled him, and he greeted the sky with a deep, piercing cry. He hadn't realized how miserable he'd been, trying to live the life of a man, denying his truest nature. Never again.

With another full-throated cry, he turned and picked up a western tailwind.

Chapter 2

As the day grew and warmed, white sweat from the horse built beneath Fiera's thighs. She'd slid the blanket down to her waist, but it still held the heat against her. She'd thought once or twice about dropping it, but her sticky thighs proved that she would need it. Her clothes were soaked and plastered to her body, like a second skin.

Captain kept a tireless rhythm, alternating between a walk and his deep drumming gallop, always traveling north. He'd tried a trot once, but had slowed when she'd nearly bounced off him.

The scenery around them changed little. Dry sparse trees and shrubs crowded the cracked earth of the road. And always that dust cloud followed Captain's hooves. The forest was silent, songbirds long moving on in search of water. The air was tight and dry and the only things that moved within it were crows and other carrion birds and the insects that drew liquids from the bodies they found. With the famine, they'd all gotten quite fat.

Early afternoon found Fiera and Captain

approaching the outskirts of a small village called Midden. Trees and brush along the road fell away to rock enclosed flat cracked dirt that had recently been fields. The whole of the settlement circled a dried center fountain on baked earth. There were five or six houses, a mercantile, and an inn, all caked with a thick layer of dust.

Captain stopped. *Do we go around?*

We need food and rest. Let me down.

The horse obediently lowered to his knees, and she slid off his back. Her legs buckled with her weight and she fell heavily against the horse. Even riding had sapped energy from her hunger-weakened body. What she had to do now, this little bit of magic, would take almost everything she had left.

She reached around her waist for the blanket that clung there. Folding it neatly, she laid it on Captain's broad back, closed her eyes and concentrated, the finger of her right hand splayed across the cloth, her other hand resting on the side of his jaw. The magic moved slower than ever before because of her weakened condition, but she eventually felt the blanket smooth and stiffen. A straight flat piece of leather formed on Captain's face.

Fiera opened her eyes and viewed her work. Instead of the blanket, a faded and scratched brown soldier's saddle sat strapped on Captain's back and a scuffed bridle circled his magnificent head.

She still had more magic to do. Turning her attention to the hard-packed road, she scuffed where she leaned against the horse until she uncovered a small stone the size to fit in the palm of her hand. She picked it up and pulled herself into the saddle; if she didn't mount now, she doubted she'd be able to afterward.

As Captain heaved to his feet, she began a slow slide to the left that she was powerless to stop. Try as she might, she hadn't the strength to pull herself upright.

17

Captain!

He swung his massive head against her hip, pushing until she was safely ensconced where she belonged. He began to walk toward Midden. *You need rest.*

I have to finish this first. Fiera again closed her eyes, concentrating on the stone. Time lengthened as she waited for her magic to begin its work. Slowly, a tickling that began deep within her reached to her palm where the rock took on a gold hue. It flattened into a shiny gold coin. Tucking it into her waistband, she tangled one hand in Captain's mane, reaching through to his silky neck. With her other hand, she grabbed a lock of her own hair and concentrated.

Nothing happened. There was no familiar drawing on her, no pulling of energy; what she had left was so little to give.

She pushed her magic as hard as she could. Sweat beaded across her face and trickled down her skin. Blackness crowded the edge of her mind. She bit her lip hard. Pain spread through her like a fire and her magic surged, changing both her hair and Captain to a sudden mousey brown.

She slumped against the pommel of the saddle. That was it. She was completely played out now. There was no more to be done, no more that she could do. Her hand was still tangled in her mount's mane. At least, this way she'd stay in her seat.

Captain shook his head. *I don't like this color.*

It's only until we get away from here. Then, I'll change you back.

If you can change my color, make a saddle from cloth and a coin from stone, why do you not make food?

Because, my friend, a stone that looks like an apple is still a stone and dirt that tastes like roast mutton is still just mud. And neither one of us can live

18

on stones, sticks, and mud.

Captain bobbed his head toward the stones lining the road. *You could make a whole treasury of gold.*

While we travel, it will work, but it will be just a matter of time before someone figures out that coin isn't as soft as real gold.

He fell into silence, waggling his ears back and forth while he seemed to consider her words. Fiera closed her eyes, fighting the black dizziness that crowded her. It pulled at her, even as the magic had, but it felt as if it had a tone of finality to it. Fear crawled across her. If she gave in to her desire to sleep, would she wake again?

She heard her horse's hoofbeats change from that of a flat dull thud on the dirt road, to a hollow clomp on wood planking. Then the world darkened outside her closed eyelids and she heard voices raised in a great and loud commotion.

When she opened her eyes, the movement around her was too busy, the light too faint for her to focus. A face came into view, really just two steady blue eyes, accompanied by an overpowering waft of perfume. Fiera drew her coin out of her waistband and held it in front of those eyes.

"Help me." Fiera's words came out so soft, she wondered for a moment if the woman had heard her. Then the coin was snatched from her hand and a shrill voice ordered, "Get her down. My lord, she's just a twig. Get that horse out of here! You there, clear that table. Fetch her some soup!"

****

For hours, Efar had flown high above the ground, his wingtips brushing against the clouds. No need to scare people. With the eagle's eyesight, he'd

19

watched fields, cottages, wagons, and farmers go by in their daily life. At first, he hadn't noticed the drought over the land below him; the change in the green of the vegetation was so gradual. It wasn't until he came across the first tree hosting dried, brown leaves that he'd taken notice. He'd carved a large arc in the sky, comparing the landscape in every direction.

Behind him, east, the forest had gradually turned greener the further back he went. To the north and south, the farmers struggled to keep their farms growing. But, traveling west again, he'd seen nothing but empty farmhouses, barren fields, and leafless trees. The people here had abandoned hope; very few were on the roads. There were no wild animals whatsoever.

His good mood dashed, he'd continued on for another hour. The road he'd been following curved north, slicing through bleak land that stretched as far as he could see. He smelled fresh rain on the ground, but it would take a lot of rains to erase the damage he saw. It sobered him. While he'd been living in the thick of a farmer's riches, these people had been starving. Graves dotted the hillsides as a testament to that.

The road led to what looked to be a small village of six or so buildings. He was about to fly past it, but he spied a tiny sign in the shape of a horse on one of the central buildings. An inn.

He hesitated, considering. The parched air *had* made him thirsty.

Efar pulled his wings behind him and dove for the wooded ground outside the village. He'd need coins and clothing. He rarely had trouble finding something to wear. As for coins, he didn't know a single inn in the world that wasn't open to a small game of chance. Though, as a dust cloud surrounded him at landing, he thought he might find the pickings a little thin for most gambling.

He shifted to human form and began looking for shirt, pants, and shoes. He couldn't very well walk into the inn naked.

The first cottage he approached had a woman visible through the windows. He skirted wide around it. It was at the second that luck blessed him. No one was home. It was a single room dwelling and, by the corner bed, he found a pair of carefully folded dark brown pants. Further investigation brought him a heavily worn shirt from a mending basket. It gave his conscience a pang to take clothing from people so destitute. But, he'd only be using them a short time.

He could go without shoes. No one would take a second glance at it; most farmers could only afford one pair per person, if that. But, he wasn't quite willing to give up yet. Checking first to see that no one was watching, Efar crept out the door and around the side of the cottage. He checked the next building to find it a blacksmith shop. The smith was working at the forge, striking his heavy hammer against a piece of white hot metal on the anvil. The scent of burnt dust and singed hair hung heavy on the air. An extra pair of muddy boots sat just inside the door.

When the smith turned and dunked his creation in his bucket, murky, stagnant water slopped onto the boots he wore. Efar reached his arm inside the doorway, snatched up the spare boots, and snuck into the woods where he dug the dried smith clay off with a stick. The boots were a bit too big, he shrugged, but it was better being than too small. He bounced on his toes experimentally and, nodding, strode toward the inn, slumping his shoulders to blend in.

****

Fiera raised a shaking spoon filled with briny

Oxblood soup. Putting it to her mouth, she slowly sipped, energy pouring through her body. Her ears rang with each shot of adrenaline and her mouth sweetened with the taste. Her pulse quickened. There was only one way that the soup could work so quickly: magic! But there had never been rumor of another witch so close to her home.

She surreptitiously searched the faces of those seated at large round tables in the dim room, mostly men in small groups, all with long, sad expressions and tankards of thin ale. The matronly woman who had helped her stood near the door to the kitchen and held her coin up to the light, staring at it with narrowed suspicious eyes. There was one other woman, young and flirting dangerously with a fat man seated in the corner. Other than a few curious glances, they all ignored Fiera now that the excitement was over. None of them gave the slightest bit of acknowledgement of her abilities, nor did she feel any magic among them.

Someone in the kitchen, then?

Voices rose from the table behind her. The first was gruff and old. "Look, I'm just saying that having water won't make that much difference. We'd still give almost everything we raise to our Lord Baldric."

The second, young and impetuous. A snort. "Of course it will make a difference. We'd be able to raise enough to pay our taxes. You know as well as I that during fat years, the taxes don't hurt as much."

"We have more lean years than fat."

"Lately. You're right." Then a whisper. "I can barely feed my family. And yet that girl..."

"Where do you suppose she got that gold coin and a horse like that?" The voices fell into sullen silence. Their stares bored holes into her back.

Time had run out quickly.

Captain, can you hear me? Where are you?

22

I'm here. In the stable behind the inn.
We need to leave.
Already? What did you do?

The door in front of her darkened as a hulking man, bent from years of hard labor, probably in the fields, paused to let his eyes adjust from the brightness outside to the dim interior of the inn. Fiera, sensing her best chance to escape, lifted her bowl and swallowed the last dregs of the soup. With energy surging through her blood, she stood and stumbled across the floor, feigning the weakness that had been upon her just moments ago. As one, the eyes of every occupant in the room followed her progress. She said to Captain, *I'll tell you later. Just be ready.*

And exactly how do I do that? I can't saddle myself and I can't unlatch this stall.

The farmer stepped off the door lintel and, as he moved into the room with heavy steps, all eyes shifted from her and followed his progress. The matron tucked the shiny coin in her waistband and jovially stepped forward to greet him, leaving her post.

Fiera, already halfway across the floor, had a choice now. She could leave by the main door, where she'd come in, sneak around the outside of the building to where Captain was stabled, or she could go through the kitchen, which she felt fairly certain would have a back door.

Mind made up, she dropped all pretense. With the magic-induced energy coursing through her body, she slipped behind the woman's back into the kitchen.

The room was smaller than most kitchens; she could cross it in four strides. The hearth was nothing more than a tiny bricked up hole in the wall where a pot simmered above low red coals while an old woman slumbered in a close-by chair. A few pots and ladles hung on the walls, but the two expansive sets of shelves

23

were empty but for a couple of withered root vegetables. The center table was also tiny, just big enough for a chopping block and a butcher's cleaver. On it sat a loaf of bread, mold on one end.

Fiera felt no quickening of her magic in response to any in the room. Somehow, she'd missed someone. The scrape of chairs came from the main room of the inn, announcing that she didn't have any more time to hunt for the person who had doctored her soup. Grabbing the loaf of bread, rock hard, she bolted around the center table and out the open back door into a small courtyard. To her left was an open shelter with two stalls, Captain in one and a broken-down, grizzled black in the other.

She rushed over and opened Captain's stall door: a simple board slid through a gap. Snatching up her saddle and bridle, she laid them on his wide back, willing them to be fastened in their proper places. In a snap, they were where they belonged. She smiled grimly; it had been a long time since she'd been strong enough that her magic had worked like it should.

As several shouting men burst through the door from the inn kitchen, Fiera sprang into the saddle with her stolen bread and Captain reared, lunging into a gallop. They raced past the men, all with gaped mouths, around the corner and up the narrow urine-stinking space between the inn and the next house, toward the main square.

Ahead of them, at the end of the alley, a young girl stepped out, a traveling cloak wrapped around her shoulders and a heavy bag hanging from one shoulder. She stared straight at the oncoming duo.

Fiera's magic surged within her, answering the same call from the small body in front of her.

The girl raised her arm straight up, hand open. As they rode past, and without any hesitation, Fiera reached down from Captain, grabbed hold of the girl's hand and pulled her aboard, behind the saddle.

Two small arms slid around Fiera's waist as Captain broke onto the center square of the village. He dug his hooves into the hard-packed dirt and turned north in an explosion of dust, leaving Midden.

Chapter 3

Efar turned in a circle. With the exception of a dapper, large-bellied man in the back of the room who struggled to his feet with the bar girl's help and followed the action, the room was empty.

He frowned. Someone had shouted, "She's gone!" and every man had coursed through the kitchen door after the disappeared girl, chairs falling to the inn's rock floor with sharp bangs. He knew to whom they referred. He'd seen her, thin as a reed, probably no more than twelve or thirteen, when he first came in, shuffling across the floor. Of course, he'd inadvertently helped her escape, drawing every eye after him as he entered into the room, while she slipped away behind him.

He didn't like mobs, and this group had given every indication of becoming one. With the griffin's extra-sensitive ears, he'd heard the murmurs of dissent before he'd pushed open the door of the inn. Even the caged whispers had been audible to him, though not the words.

It had come as no surprise, then, to see the desperation written so plainly in the girl's green eyes when he'd finally stepped into the building. The malevolence on the faces of four of the six inhabitants had shocked him, though. Why would they want to hurt a small starving girl?

Efar shrugged. It wasn't his problem. And, it worked in his benefit. His family was all too well known, and he didn't really want to be recognized.

He smiled at the bar girl, and then reached for the pitcher of ale sitting on the shelved wall. As he turned his attention back to her, he crooked his finger, beckoning her to join him. She swayed her hips as she strolled up to him with a seductive smile, as he knew she would. Not many women resisted him. The barmaid took his hand, and let him lead her out the front door.

Hoofbeats thundered out of town, a giant cloud of dust billowing in their wake. Efar slipped away with the barmaid.

Strolling through the bare trees and scuffing in the leaves, they came to a wide fallen oak where they sat. Efar gulped from the tankard of ale, watching the barmaid out of the corner of his eye. He put down the ale, smacked his lips, and smiled. "What's your name?"

"Dulcette, sir." She leaned toward him. In the light of day, he now saw that she was nothing but a child. Bits of cloth peeked out the bosom of her dress and the hip that rested against him was too soft to be real flesh and bone.

"Well, Dulcette, what's your age?"

She leaned closer. "I'm fourteen, sir." She sat quietly, waiting on him, as she probably had other customers of the inn, waiting for him to decide how he wanted to use her. Her promising smile guaranteed him a night's distraction, but he wasn't sure he wanted that any longer. His heart wanted more. It wanted to be in love. Taking her had been an impulse, something he had done many times. A habit.

Men of the area had the saying "Old enough to wed, old enough to bed." While it was true the Church sanctioned marriage for twelve year old girls, Efar wanted someone with more curves, someone who knew her own mind and wasn't afraid to speak it.

Abruptly, he stood, took Dulcette's hand, and pulled her to her feet. "I have no money to pay you. Go back to your mistress."

She stared in his eyes a moment. "I could stay..."

He shook his head firmly, now more certain than ever. He didn't want her. He wanted someone he hadn't met yet. "Go back to the fat man. He'll pay well for you. If you treat him kindly, he may decide he can't do without you." He gave her a gentle shove in the right direction.

Biting her lip, she glanced back at him and then picked a path through the dead undergrowth, swaying her hips gently.

Efar shook his head. He really *was* a fool.

Backtracking to the cottage where he'd found the clothes, he undressed, folding and neatly laying them on the steps. Then he moved off into the woods again and shifted.

****

Bartheleme stared out the open stone window at the party of dragons flying toward the castle. Centermost of those was a serpentine female the color of pine trees: the woman he'd be taking as queen. Her coloring, coupled with his brighter emerald green, guaranteed beautiful children. She was a strong woman who would support him well when he succeeded to the crown. Furthermore, her family held the English coastal lands directly north of his father's, east all the way to the mid-mountains. It was a good pairing for everyone.

But, it was an impromptu visit. And very

inconvenient for him.

With a deep sigh, he turned away, coming face-to-face with his twin sister, Cecily. As was her usual, she wore her black hair coiffed high on her head. She watched him closely with brown eyes that seemed to know every truth he hid. "You think to slip away?"

He shrugged. "I have things that need attention." Like a meeting with his father's agent.

She narrowed her eyes and propped her hands on her hips. She spoke in his mind. *Like what, exactly?*

He didn't answer. There were things pressing in his life at the moment, but he couldn't tell a soul. So, it appeared he did nothing. Everyone in the whole castle mocked his apparent uselessness. Except his sister.

Cecily nodded and said aloud, "Tell me and don't lie."

Anger flared within him. Fire leapt to his cheeks. He reached inside him, to the dragon, growing in size and girth as he shifted, gasping at the spikes of pain that lanced through his bones from changing so quickly. In front of him, Cecily shifted too. Though they were twins and nearly identical as humans, that wasn't true as dragons. Whereas his was emerald green and thickly muscled, her body was lithe and, as the sun glinted off them, her scales were the blue of sparkling sapphires.

They stumbled back from each other, nearly dropping to battle positions. There was a reason the castle had such vaulted ceilings. Then Cecily straightened. *No, Bartheleme. I won't fight you. I'm just saying you can't hide the truth from me.*

He knew she was right; his heart spoke to the truth of that. She was always right and it normally drove him nuts. This time, however, it only left him thinking. She might be able to help him with his escape problem. *Father has set me a task, not knowing these people were arriving. How can I do that, trapped here?*

29

She rubbed her head against his. *If you ask me, I'll help you get away with no one seeing you. But don't tell me where you go. I want to be honest with Father and his guests when he interrogates me.*

Help me, then.

She jutted her nose toward the distant line of trees. *Stay here until night. Then, go on foot through there. Once you're on the other side, shift and fly away. I'll tell the guests you've already left.* She whirled and, in an instant, had shifted back to human. She snatched up one of the many robes strategically placed throughout the castle and rushed from the room.

He turned for one last look out the window at the final arriving guests. Leave it to his sister to be his salvation.

****

Fiera pushed Captain to put as many paces between them and Midden as possible, but it was long after dark when they, at last, came to a crossroads. *We should rest here tonight and pick up in the morning. We'll be able to tell our choices better by then.*

Running blind in the beginning had worked well for them, until Midden, but now Fiera realized they needed to make rational decisions. Faced with three directions to go, three choices, neither she nor Captain could decide which to take. Exhaustion numbed their minds.

Captain backtracked to a widening in the road, a small cul-de-sac. The woods there were deep and dark, with brown-needled pines and conifers mixing in with the bare hardwoods. And, as always, the ground was cracked and hard-packed with thirst. The girl behind the saddle hadn't said a word since her rescue. Fiera decided the child was near eight years old. Not old enough to be on her own. She shook her head at herself. Now she was

30

forced to become the girl's babysitter. She would drop her at the next city. What had she been thinking?

But she knew the answer to that: she had responded to the magic within the girl because she was tired of being alone, tired of hiding from everyone, tired of pretending to be...anything but what she really was: a witch.

They dismounted. Fiera stood tall and stretched, but the small girl laid down her bag, more of a patched cloth that looked as if it had been a hat of some kind, with two holes cut into it for handles, and scurried into the woods. Fiera eyed her speculatively and reached for the bag. What the child had in there might give a clue to her nature. But, hand in midair above the cut-out handles, she hesitated, and then withdrew. If the shoe were on the other foot, if it were her bag, she wouldn't want anyone snooping.

The young girl returned with sticks, dead leaves, and dried pine needles, which she arranged on the ground in a kind of small, pointed structure, the softer dry stuff beneath the sticks. From a fold in her cloak, she removed a flint and a stone. She repeatedly struck these together at the base of the structure, spilling sparks onto the leaves and needles. In no time at all, they had a tiny fire burning. The child disappeared back into the woods, but returned a moment later with an armful of stout branches that she broke and laid across the fire.

Fiera fetched the loaf of bread she'd stowed beneath the pommel of the saddle for easy carrying and laid it by the fire. Returning to Captain, she reached for his bridle. Instantly, the girl was there, gently pushing at her hands. Startled, Fiera let go and stepped back. The child pulled the big horse's head lower and unbuckled the bridle.

Fiera moved to the saddle, and once again the girl pushed her away. Fiera said, "I'm taller and it'll be easier for me to do this."

The girl's face clouded with a deep frown and a harsh downturn to her mouth. She shook her head violently, dislodging the cap of her cloak to show a mass of brown curls. Stepping up next to the saddle, she effectively shoved Fiera out of the way.

Perplexed, Fiera returned to the fire. What was going on? Did the girl think she had to do these things to pay for her rescue? Or was it simply a gesture of thanks? Well, she wouldn't be so thankful when she was abandoned in the next city.

Fiera waited while the young girl finished unsaddling Captain, rubbed him with the hem of her cloak, and returned to the fire. Digging in her bag, the child brought out another loaf of rock hard bread, a full wheel of yellow cheese, a bowl, an earthen bottle, and a long, dangerous kitchen knife. Reaching once more into the bag, she fished around the bottom and then pulled out a handful of oats. Rising again, she walked to Captain and held her hand beneath the horse's nose.

Captain spoke in Fiera's mind. *I like her. Let's keep her.*

We'll make that decision once we get to know her better. Though, in truth, Fiera had already made it.

I know her. She brought oats for me. Something you forgot.

I was in a hurry. People were chasing me. I'm sorry. She thought that would end the conversation, but she was wrong.

You remembered food for yourself.

It was in the open, on my way to the door. I'm sorry. Was she really defending her actions to a horse?

The oats were in a bag right by my saddle.

I said, I'm sorry. I don't know what else I can say. I didn't see it. I promise that, from now on, I'll make sure you have plenty.

32

It would have only taken a few more seconds to grab some.

Captain! As the horse lapsed into blessed silence, Fiera pinched the bridge of her nose and closed her eyes. Rebuked by a horse. She could have laughed at it.

Sensing movement by her side, she opened her eyes and saw the girl had seated herself by the fire and was pressing the long knife into the yellow cheese wheel. Might as well get started learning about her right away.

"What's your name? I'm Fiera."

The girl pretended she didn't hear, but her head lowered a little more over her task, hacking at the cheese more than cutting it.

Fiera tried again. "What's your name?"

When she received that same non-response, she reached over and gently cupped the child's chin in her hand. Raising her head so that their gazes could meet, she asked, "Do you have a name?"

The girl shook her head and sudden tears spilled down her face. She pulled her chin out of Fiera's hand and re-focused on the cheese. With a final, savage chop, a butter-colored slice separated from the wheel. The girl picked it up and handed it to Fiera with a chunk of bread.

Fiera's heart turned heavy. No name. Her anger blazed at the bar matron in Midden, suddenly glad she'd duped her with a coin and had stolen from her. How could a child grow up like that? How could she gain a sense of identity? Independence? It was nearly impossible, and yet, this small girl somehow had. "When I was young, about your age, I had a sister named Marie. May I call you that?"

The little head, still bowed over the knife and the next slice of cheese, slowly nodded.

"Good. Now, let's have a rule. I want to do things around our camp. I'll do the heavy things. And the tall ones. You do the light ones and the shorter ones. Does that sound fair to you? We'll be a team, taking care of each other and Captain."

Marie dropped her knife and flung her arms around Fiera in a tight hug. When she pulled away, only seconds later, and with a sheepish smile, tears once again streamed down her face.

"Where are you from?" The novelty of being with another witch sparked a million questions within Fiera, but when the girl scowled again, she gave up and concentrated on her food. Perhaps later.

Chapter 4

As a griffin, Efar rose into the night sky and headed north. He took his time, reveling in the chilly air against his face and under his wings. Flying in the clear moonlight thrilled him. The pitcher of ale he'd finished off swaddled his head in a thick layer of cotton. He hadn't a care in the world.

His eagle eyes didn't have the night sight of the nocturnal owl, but, because of the lion in him, he could still see well enough if he flew a bit closer to the ground. The road he followed twisted and turned around huge outcroppings of boulders and a gorge that had been, in wetter years, a wide river, but was only sand and stone now. The leafless treetops pointed fiercely up at him like daggers or stakes in a hunting pit.

It wasn't long before he passed over a tiny campfire, now embers, by the side of the road. Swooping low, he took a better look. Two small forms, probably children, lay on opposite sides of the fire. Both thrashed and jerked in fitful dreams. The shadow of a great draft horse loomed behind the smallest body.

Slowly, it dropped to its knees and lay behind it, touching it with its nose. The child calmed into a deep, quiet sleep within seconds. The other person dreamed and thrashed on.

Efar circled. His heart cried for the quiet presence a campfire with strangers, even children, might afford him. He'd spent far too much time sitting on that log in Midden, drinking ale and feeling sorry for himself after Dulcette had left. That made him thrice a fool. First, for leaving Gabrielle. Then, for turning away Dulcette. Finally, for pining over a woman he'd never met and might not even exist.

He looked down at the campers again. He could drop into the woods and spend the rest of the night close to them, or he could fly back to Midden, pick up his clothes, return, and join the campers in person.

As he circled again, trying to make up his mind, the horse below lifted its head and stared at him. Spell broken, Efar banked toward the stars and flew on.

The road below widened into a crossroads. He continued straight on. Occasional campfires dotted the roadside. Within two hours of flying, he noticed that the trees there held some of their leaves. This forest, not afflicted as heavily by drought, only darkened more as he flew north.

Groups of shadows darker than those of the trees darted out from the security of the leaf-covered forest from campfire to campfire. Highwaymen! There had to be twenty or thirty of them, all working in groups of four or five. Fires here and there flickered, sparked, and went out. Seconds later, shapes lurked away.

Directly below him, robbers materialized at an unsuspecting camp. Angling his wings back, Efar dove for the ground. Before he even landed, he was reaching for the first robber. With one rake of his eagle claw, he disabled the man. Leaving him writhing and dying on the ground, Efar snapped at a second thief with his great beak, crushing the man's shoulder. The robber ran away, clutching his arm close to his side, following two loot-bearing companions.

Efar looked around the campsite. He'd arrived too late. All traces of the camp had been swept away. Searching the sparse underbrush, he found the campers' lifeless bodies couched beneath, hidden from the world. The fire had been buried in the soft loam of the roadside, the ground still warm to the touch. He changed to human form and hid the now dead robber with the others in the shrubs.

Sorrow filled him and he thought of the children camped on the other side of the crossroads. Somehow, he'd managed to bond with them, though they were oblivious to it. He couldn't leave them to this fate.

Cursing himself, he undressed the body most closely his size and, clothes clutched in his claws, flew back toward the tiny campfire with the giant horse.

****

Fiera's dream that night was a quiet and soulless one, the kind a person had when she hid herself so long and so thoroughly that she no longer knew herself. It was a falling dream. The ground gave way beneath her feet, and she fell into a cavern, down and down and down, deep into the swallowing earth, flailing her arms, kicking, and silently screaming. There was no bottom; she just kept falling.

She woke, her face and body slick with a familiar sweat. Staring at the bright gems of stars in the velvet black of night, she struggled to calm the frantic beat of her heart. The warm night wind brushed across her, cooling her. How many times had she had that very same nightmare? How many times had she awakened alone, crying for someone to accept her, magic and all? She'd thought, since striking out on her own and no longer hiding, that the bad dreams would have stopped.

With a deep shaking sigh, she turned on her side, facing the dying fire. The girl, Marie, was curled on the far side, like a caterpillar in the spring. Captain lay on his chest beside the child, his nose resting against her hip in a show of solidarity.

The night before had been emotionally traumatic for the child. Fiera had tried to keep the mood light, chattering about nothing much at all, but Marie's quiet had broken into quick storms of tears and hard hugs. Eventually she fell into an exhausted sleep curled up on the opposite side of the fire.

Fiera smiled. No, she wasn't alone. Not anymore. There was no need to hide what she was any longer. For either of them. She let herself drift off to a deep sleep that remained untroubled until the first rays of dawn lit her face.

Opening her eyes once again, she stretched and looked over at Marie. The girl still slept in her caterpillar pose, softly snoring, but Captain had moved away. He stood several yards behind her, sniffing at a patch of dead and dried grass that had grown beneath the long outstretched arm of an old oak, now bare as if in the dead of winter. As his muzzle brushed across the grass, brittle from lack of water, the blades broke off, shattering into dozens of tiny pieces. He licked the ground, trying to catch up the tiny shards. His breaths raised miniature dust clouds all around him.

Fiera rose and reached for Marie's bag. First, she removed the knife, cheese, and bread, and then she scooped out a large handful of grain and carried it over to Captain. Cupping both hands together, she let the oats spread in a wider space to accommodate the width of the horse's mouth. *I'm sorry, you're on short rations until we can get more.*

He shuffled his soft lips across her hands, gently shoveling the oats into his mouth. *Well, if you hadn't forgotten --*

Don't start! I'm in a good mood and I don't want it ruined. We'll get more oats at the next village.

I don't think we should go into any more villages. People don't seem to like you.

We have no choice, my friend. While Marie and I have her doctored Oxblood soup to drink, you need water. We'll need to get going soon before someone comes along who might recognize us.

Captain lapsed into silence. He concentrated his tongue on the remaining oats that hid between Fiera's fingers.

The sound of movement came from the direction of the fire. Captain pivoted his ears, and then he lifted his long nose and looked.

Fiera followed his gaze. Marie, still sound asleep, was thrashing her arms and legs, scraping them on the ground as if fighting or running in a nightmare.

Fiera wiped the few remaining kernels of oats from her hands and ran toward the girl. She dropped to her knees beside the child and reached to take her in her arms. Marie sat bolt upright, screaming in a low, guttural voice, her mouth a black yawning hole, with only a stump for a tongue.

Fiera caught her breath, tears filling her eyes, suddenly understanding the girl's silence. Someone, somewhere, had cut out her tongue! Sliding her arms around Marie's tiny form, Fiera tried to pull her close. The girl, however, pushed against Fiera and, with her face flaming red, she jumped to her feet and raced into the woods, twigs and underbrush cracking where she went.

"Marie!" Fiera scrambled upright and followed,

but the girl was fast and was soon lost from sight. Clambering on top of a fallen and partially rotted tree, Fiera scanned the skeleton woods. Nothing moved.

From the road, Captain called, *I smell someone coming!*

She frowned, not taking her gaze from the task of finding Marie. *How far away?*

There still is some time. They're down the road a piece, yet. Around the bend. A single rider. Smells like that black that was next to me in Midden. Stinky fellow.

You need to hide in the forest right away! Find a big fallen tree and lie down behind it. Get as low as you can. For answer, Fiera heard the crashing of something huge moving in the woods off to her left. She dashed back to their camp and gathered the knife and food into the hat-bag. Scuffing her feet, she covered the fire with dirt from the road. Then she snatched up the saddle and bridle, pushing her magic into them and changing them back to a blanket.

Fiera bolted to the safety of the forest and the log she'd been standing upon earlier. Before she dropped to the ground, she took one more good look around for Marie. Still nothing.

With a deep sigh, Fiera jumped down from the fallen tree and hunkered behind it. To the north, behind a similar tree, Captain lay on his chest, his neck stretched as long as possible and his jaws on the ground.

The forest of dying trees was silent, yet within seconds of settling into her hiding place, small arms snaked around her waist and Marie squeezed her tight. Fiera hugged her just as strong. She placed her finger to her lips, pointing to the road with the index finger of her other hand. The girl nodded.

Relief at Marie's safe return rolled through Fiera, but she had to be honest, it wasn't just for the girl's sake. It had a lot to do with her nightmare and her loneliness. She just didn't want to be alone anymore. She sighed deeply and glanced down at her young charge leaning against her. No. She couldn't abandon Marie anywhere.

They didn't have to wait long before the grizzled black horse, easy to see through the stark tree trunks, ambled down the road. The flirting fat man from the back corner of the inn in Midden rode, hunched low, watching the ground. When they reached the wayside area and the camp, the man stopped the black. He stared at the smoke eking through the dirt and the scuffs beside it. He lifted his head and roved his gaze over the stark forest.

Fiera held her breath and glanced over at Captain. *Be absolutely still. He's looking this way.*

Who? The horse?

Fiera squinched her eyes shut tight, working to control her exasperation. After a second, she opened her eyes again. *Why would I be worried about a horse?*

I don't know. You're the one who said it.

I didn't... She stopped and shook her head. Now wasn't the time for an argument. *Just be still for a few more minutes.*

Ducking lower, she peeked through the rotting branches of the log to watch the fat man. Who was he? What did he want with them?

****

The early morning sun stretched through bare branches and reached the forest floor, waking Efar from his most recent catnap. He'd decided to keep watch from a hollow between some clusters of brown-needled spruces in the woods on the other side of the road and downwind from the children. He'd opted not to join them, for fear of frightening them. Nor did he need the horse smelling him.

Though it had been dark when he arrived, skulking from shadow to shadow, and his view had been partly obscured, he thought the bigger child was a young girl. She could be tempting for many travelers, highwaymen or not.

Stretching his neck to peer above the plane of the forest floor, he saw a fat man on an old black standing still as death beside the campfire. The children and their horse were nowhere to be seen. Had they slipped away in the predawn hours? Efar lifted his nose, using his lion's sense of smell, and sucked in a great draft of air. The reek of the black horse all but drowned out any other scents. He knew that odor: dragons. Many of them traveled the land, exploring, much like him. Perhaps this horse, then, had belonged to one of them. From the strength of the scent, the dragon had owned it for quite a while, maybe even raised it. Did the rider know? Did he work for the dragon families?

Apparently reaching some decision, the rider slowly left the camp. Sniffing in short breaths with his mouth open, Efar was able to better taste the other scents of the forest. Two humans and one other horse were hidden somewhere nearby.

Satisfied, Efar crept on stealthy feet after the horse and rider, careful to stay behind the security of the close-growing tree trunks. The heavy man in the saddle had been at the inn. It wouldn't be unusual for a traveler to come this way, but why had he shown so much interest in the campfire? With slicked back hair, tailored clothes and a thick fob chain across his wide belly, he had the look of a paid informant, searching for someone. The children?

The fat man stopped the horse at a crossroads and studied the ground. He looked down one branch of the cross road and then the other. Finally, he lifted his head and stared down the road straight ahead. After a long moment, he turned the horse to the left and rode away.

Efar emerged from the trees and waited at the crossroads for a long time to ensure the informant wouldn't double back. When that didn't happen, he returned to a rock within the confines of the dried up roadside brush and settled down to wait for the children.

Highwaymen straight ahead and the fat informant to the west. That left only one direction for the children to take. He had to convince them to go east.

****

Fiera waited, Marie by her side, with Captain's brown bulk hidden behind another nearby fallen log. Silence filled the forest. She barely dared to breathe for fear the fat man on the black horse might reappear and find them hiding among the empty trees.

Slowly, she stood, craning her neck to view the road through the bare tree trunks. *Captain, do you still smell them?*

His voice resounded in her head, *The horse is gone.*

The man, too?

Gone.

Still, she crept slowly, placing her feet in the dried leaves and twigs with care. Marie followed like a shadow. From behind the other giant log, Captain struggled to his feet and shook himself.

Reaching the tree line, Fiera checked both directions for anyone approaching. The dry, flat road was empty. The fat man was, indeed, gone. She propped her hands on her hips and viewed the other two with a critical eye. "Well, that was close. How about we change our colors again?"

43

She placed her hand on Captain's brown coat and concentrated. White hairs appeared in an all over irregular pattern. His mane and tail turned salt and pepper and black appeared on his legs, just above his hooves. Stepping back, she viewed her handiwork. What had once been a proud, albeit boring, brown war horse was now a flea-bitten draft.

Captain shook his head and his voice rumbled in her mind. *This isn't my normal color and it isn't an improvement over the last.*

It's only temporary. I promise.

You promised to change me back.

I will, but we're still not safe yet. Turning to Marie, she asked, "Do you think you could pretend to be a boy for a little while?"

Eyes wide, the girl slowly nodded.

Fiera brushed her hand across Marie's soft curls, turning them blond in the wake. She gripped the child's dress, as well as her own, and turned them to boy's clothing. Marie's facial features were a bit soft for a boy, but there was nothing to be done about that. She pointed at the girl's feet. "No shoes. Rub a little dirt across your face, like you were wiping sweat. And tie your cloak around your waist so it's not so noticeable what it is."

Fiera transformed the shoes to two worn flop caps such as she'd seen boys wear. She changed her own hair color to match Marie's, shortening it to just above her shoulders. She also rubbed dirt on her cheeks. For the first time, her emaciated body worked for her. They would look like two farm kids visiting the city on the family draft horse. No one would give them another thought.

The smoke from the buried fire had finally died away and she was loath to make another, so they ate a quick breakfast of cold Oxblood soup and bread.

44

Marie watched Fiera out of the corner of her eye until they finished eating and were packing up. Then she placed her hand on Captain's side, much the way Fiera had, and, with her other hand, she made like she was tossing something straight up in the air.

Fiera frowned. "Are you asking about my magic?"

The girl gave a huge nod.

"Well, I have two gifts. I can speak with animals in my mind and I can change the form of things, but not the basic composition." She picked up the lard-thickened blanket Marie had slept on and laid it against the horse's jaw. Pushing her magic into it, the cloth became a rope bridle. There would be no saddle this time. Real farm kids didn't usually have one for their draft animals. Then she took a handful of dust from the road, packing it in her hand, and changing it into a flat silver coin.

"My creations are only as solid as what I start with. That bridle holds because it was a strong blanket. But this coin," Fiera tapped the silver disc and it crumbled, "is still just dust."

She shrugged and wiped the silver dirt from her fingers. "What is your magic?"

Marie sadly shook her head. Her arms hung lifeless at her sides, as if she were embarrassed at the inability to produce something.

"But, you *do* have magic! I can feel it. You put energy in the soup. You saved my life!"

For answer, Marie lifted a flap on a hidden pouch tied around her waistline. Inside were more than a dozen tiny packets of powders, grains, and dried leaves.

"Potions? Who taught you?"

Again, the girl shook her head. She shrugged.

"Don't you think that's magic, knowing those things without being taught?" Fiera clambered aboard

45

Captain and reached down for Marie, pulling her up behind. "I've heard of witches studying all their lives and they still weren't able to produce anything near the power in that soup."

Another thought hit her. "There's only one way you could teach yourself that quickly. I'll bet you can pick up a strange plant and you know its properties. That's magic. And I think it's amazing." She glanced behind her and was rewarded with Marie's pleased grin.

Captain turned them toward the crossroads. He said, *You could make her a new tongue from her own flesh.*

I wish I could, but I can't manipulate living things. That's why hair comes back in as the original color: it's living at the root, but not the shaft.

Pity. Wings would have been nice.

They traveled in silence until they came to the crossroads. The trip went a lot quicker than Fiera remembered from the night before. Startled, she turned and stared down the road in the direction they'd come. From her vantage point on Captain's back, she could make out the beginning of the wayside where they'd spent the night. It wasn't as far away as she'd thought. Any traveler could have seen them. No wonder the fat man had found them so easily. It was just as well they'd gotten an early start and changed their colors.

Turning to the crossroads again, she frowned, facing the dilemma of which direction to go. There were no signs, nor markers of any kind. She didn't see a soul to ask. "What do you think, Marie? Which way to a city big enough that we can buy water for Captain?"

Captain answered, *You know what I think.*

I didn't ask you. Be quiet.

The girl peered around from behind. After a moment of twisting, turning, and bumping Fiera, she pointed to the road directly across from them. She then

46

held her small hands together as if praying, but pulled them open.

Fiera took her turn twisting and staring at all three choices. Then she nodded. "You're right. That road *is* wider. It's got to lead to a city."

She spoke to the horse. *Captain, hollow your back and hang your head more. Drag your feet. You're supposed to be a tired, lumbering draft horse.*

I hate this. But, he did as she asked.

A niggling worry built with her. That fat man on the black had definitely been looking for them. And now, he was probably headed towards the city, as well, on the very same road!

****

Efar sat on a flat slab of rock behind a cluster of dried up pine scrub. Every time he moved, brown needles scattered to the ground. From his vantage point, he watched the children make up their minds which direction to go. He'd decided not to interfere unless they went the wrong way. They sat bareback on their giant horse, bare feet swinging free, caps pulled low on their heads, every bit the picture of farm boys. The rope bridle was worn and scuffed, the children's clothes equally so.

Minds made up, they started down the northern road, the one leading to the city and the highwaymen. He stood and stepped through the empty branches into view. As one, both children and the horse jerked their heads toward him, their eyes wide with alarm. He held up his hands to show that he meant no harm. "That's a dangerous road."

As he approached, the horse jigged sideways away from him. Stopping ten feet away, Efar waited while the oldest boy pulled the creature back under control.

The child faced him, piercing him with eyes the color of green olives. "What kind of danger?" His voice was low and still like a deep pool. He turned and searched down their intended road as if he could spot the evil lurking there.

The boy's voice surprised Efar and he took a closer look at the child's features. Though thin and angular, the lips were full, the brow high and the eyelashes were long and sweeping. Women were one thing he knew well above all others. She'd tried to camouflage it, but she was no boy. He glanced at the child sitting behind, but because of the smaller boy's youth, it was hard to tell if he was really a boy or another girl in hiding. Some boys just plain had effeminate faces, especially when younger.

Efar returned his attention to the masquerading girl at the front of the horse and tried to imagine her as a full-grown woman. Yes, he was sure. All the angles and features fit that of a woman. One with a voice like that could go a long way in soothing a man's troubles. He'd imagine she'd be well sought after when she'd grown. But she was too young for him now. "Highwaymen. You'd be better off taking the eastern road."

She again appraised him with her cool green eyes. Then she shook her head, shifting her thick blond hair and jutting her chin in the direction she was traveling. "We're going to the city. We need water for our horse." She patted her mount's neck and it bobbed its head as if in response.

It struck Efar that the girl looked familiar to him. He thought a moment, but was unable to place her. "You have a strong, healthy horse. He's bound to catch someone's attention. As if that isn't enough, you two...boys...are both the right age to be sold into slavery. Go a different direction. Surely there's water to the east."

She narrowed her eyes and pointed to the baked earth below her horse's hooves. "This road guarantees water, the other doesn't. Thank you for your concern, but we're headed to the city." She nudged the draft horse and it stepped off without a fuss.

Efar muttered under his breath, "If you even get there." She was a stubborn one.

He watched the children rock back and forth with their mount's giant strides. If he figured out they were girls, someone else could, too. Cursing himself again, he jogged to catch up. "I propose we travel together. This road isn't even safe for a single traveler like me. We can protect each other."

The girl shrugged and lifted her head in defiance, her message clear: he could do as he liked, but they didn't need him to protect them. Admirable, but foolish.

At that moment, Efar realized she was the girl from the inn. As they walked, he studied her profile and, in his mind, compared it with what he'd seen of her in that dim room. Same forehead, same desperate eyes. She was definitely the same person he had helped escape. Though he thought her remembered her hair as darker.

That explained the fat informant's interest. She must own or have taken something of value, but he'd no idea what a simple country girl could have. Efar let his gaze rove over the draft horse. It was a nice horse, something to be had, but he found it hard to believe a paid informant would be interested in a girl's mount. He turned his gaze to the boy behind her only to find the child staring boldly back at him. Boy or girl?

Efar turned his attention back to the road. He tried to remember the conversation he'd overheard through the door at the inn, but so much had been said in hushed voices.

With a sigh, he looked up at the girl, putting on

49

his most winning smile. "I suppose, if we're traveling together, it'll be easier if we know each other's names." He placed his hand on his chest. "I'm Efar."

She glanced at him, but didn't say anything for quite a few strides. Then, almost begrudgingly, she said in a tight voice, "My name is William. That's Henry behind me. This," she nodded toward the horse, "is Captain."

He nodded, encouraging her, but, after waiting a few moments, it became apparent nothing more would be forthcoming. He tried again. "I traveled from my home southeast of here, a tiny village in the mountains above Hertford. I decided to see what lay in this direction. And you? Where are you from?"

Again, she gave that bitter twist to her mouth as if swallowing a bad medicine, but her gaze suddenly hollowed, speaking a different story. "South." Then she fell silent.

Efar also lapsed into quiet. Trying to get two answers from her had nearly worn out his social skills. He'd never had to work so hard to get someone to speak to him. Obviously, she didn't want him to know anything about them.

It was going to be a long journey.

****

Through the day, Fiera kept Captain at a steady walk. They skipped the noon meal in order to get to the city quicker, the horse insisting he was fine. The silence their group maintained allowed Fiera time to think. She worried about catching up to the grizzled black and his rider, who could be ahead of her. They also needed to get water soon. Midden, the day before, had been the last place Captain had been able to drink. Fiera wanted to push him to a gallop, but that would be more

50

detrimental than helpful. He would sweat, making him even more dehydrated.

The stranger beside her, Efar, worried her, as well. She had no doubt he was the farmer who had enabled her escape from the inn in Midden; he must have crept ahead of them on the road as they slept. Though he preached against highwaymen, he could be a robber, himself. Or a rapist. Or any number of things. He could be in league with the fat man. Very glad she'd chosen to hide them as boys, she still itched to race away from him. Circumstances, however, conspired to keep them together.

She glanced over at his long, wavy, light brown hair and strong masculine face. He didn't look evil. Nor was he bad to look at. His smile came easy, and when he looked at her, his clear blue eyes seemed to dance in merriment over some secret joke. He walked assuredly, as if he knew he could handle anything that came his way. Could she trust him? If he was what he purported to be, a traveler who, by circumstance, was at the inn at the same time, then he would be an excellent guard.

When she'd changed herself and Marie to boys, she'd been thinking of becoming exactly what most people wouldn't notice. She hadn't been thinking of thieves. Though she'd made it clear to Efar they didn't need his protection, they just might.

Captain broke into her thoughts, as he had been all day, his voice strident in her mind. *I'm telling you, he doesn't smell right!* He shook his head in emphasis.

Stop telling me that and give me some details. Fiera repressed the desire to sputter her lips in frustration. He'd been going on about the smell ever since Efar had joined them. She would have thought the horse would be used to the smell by now. But then, it might not be just the stranger unsettling him. She'd noticed that as Captain grew thirstier, he became more

51

jittery.

He doesn't smell human.

What then? An animal?

None I know. I think my nose is ruined. Between him and that stinky black horse, I many never be able to smell correctly again. He jigged sideways, as Efar stretched out his hand to stroke his neck.

"Please don't," Fiera snapped at the man. "Can't you see you make him nervous?"

Efar frowned a moment, but widened the gap between them. He bowed slightly. "A thousand apologies. He's a magnificent animal." He looked up at her with crystal blue eyes. He smiled.

She felt her peevishness at him begin to melt. A warm glow sputtered to life deep inside her. She slapped the horse's shoulder. "Yes, he is. My father could always pick out the best."

He seems like a nice fellow. Maybe I could get used to his smell. Captain arched his neck and lifted his legs higher with each stride.

I'm sure you could.

Efar asked, "What did your father farm?"

What to tell him? That she didn't know? She'd never been allowed outside the house for fear someone would take issue with her red hair and green eyes. What did her mother serve on the table the most? "Cabbage and parsnips. We had a herd of goats, too."

Marie/Henry tapped her arm from behind and pointed up into the sky.

Fiera shifted her gaze to the horizon. A dark shape flew toward them against the graying light. "A bird!"

Efar's voice was dry. "It's a wren. We must be getting near the edge of this cursed dry land."

A wren! Excitement infused her, flushing her skin. Her breathing came rapidly. It had been so long

52

since she'd seen a bird of any kind. In her mind, she called out to it. *Hello, Wren! I'm happy to see you. Would you tell me what's to the north of us?*

The brown avian circled in the sky above them. In typical bird form, it skipped the greeting. *Green. Water.*

How far is the water?

A merchant sells it from his cart. A half day's ride for you.

Many thanks. Turn around and go back. You're the only bird we've seen for many months. There's nothing this way but desolation and dirt.

My thanks to you, also. The bird wheeled in the sky and flapped back the way he had come. Fiera watched him disappear.

She turned to find Efar gazing at her with an amused smile and twinkling eyes. He nodded toward the bird. "You followed every move that bird made. You love animals, don't you?"

She colored. If he only knew the truth! "I do. Any kind. But, it's been so long since we've had songbirds." She lapsed into uncomfortable silence and stared at the packed dirt road directly in front of them, unsure of where to turn the conversation.

"The wren means we're close to water, too." He reached to pat Captain, and for the first time, the horse didn't step out of range. He *did* turn his head away and blow great gusts of warm air through his nose, though.

Fiera ignored the horse's antics. "I've heard there's a merchant who sells water from his cart somewhere on this road. Perhaps we'll run into him early tomorrow."

"Did you hear that in Midden?"

She snapped her gaze to him. Behind her, Marie/Henry stiffened. The girl's arms tightened around Fiera's waist.

He laughed. "Yes, I recognize you. And I'm glad I helped you get away. That bunch didn't seem very nice. Was it your horse they were after?" He nodded at Captain.

"Yes," she answered dully. She gave him something close to the truth. "They thought I would be easy to steal from because I'm small."

He nodded and frowned, his eyes narrowing with the seriousness of his words. He spoke softly. "You're small *and* a girl. You'll discover that not all thieves hide in the woods. What's your real name?"

Before she could stop herself, Fiera blurted, "Are you a thief as well?"

His eyes flew open wide, but instead of angry words rebuking the accusation, he chuckled again. "No. I'm no robber." He smiled up at her and Marie/Henry, blue eyes dancing with mischief.

It was an infectious smile and Fiera found herself wanting to respond in kind, but she held her emotions at bay. No doubt there was more behind his simple statement, judging by his eyes, but she now felt safe with him. She felt she could trust him. At least in this. Still, she'd keep an eye on him and keep Marie's real identity hidden as long as she could. "My real name is Fiera. Is my disguise so easy to see through?"

"I've had the advantage of traveling with you in fairly close proximity, but I don't think you would be found out with just a passing glance."

"Then, I'd like to stay hidden as a boy until we get to the city."

He nodded. He was sure there was more to her reason for hiding, but he'd leave it for now.

Dusk was only getting heavier. If she were going to buy water tomorrow, that meant she had to collect stones and change them to coins without Efar seeing. She pulled on Captain's reins. "We should stop here for the night."

****

Efar stood for a moment, hands on hips, watching Fiera. While Henry—boy or girl, he'd given up trying to figure it out—had immediately taken to the woods on the eastern side of the road to gather burning material, the girl set about scuffing the cracked edges of the road after she'd cared for the horse. Occasionally, she bent low and studied what she'd found, but other times, she scooped something directly from the ground into her pocket. Finally, his curiosity got the better of him. "What do you have there?"

She looked up at him with guilt in her olive green eyes. "Rocks."

He leaned forward. Did he hear her right? "Rocks?"

She nodded and returned to her search, her thick blond hair brushing across the tops of her shoulders. "I collect them." Great clouds of dust rose from her feet to envelope her skinny body in a kind of fog. She didn't seem to notice, though.

Efar shook his head. Who in their right mind collected rocks? He liked her, but she was an odd one. Everything about her was other than what he expected: her voice, her decisiveness, her frankness, and now the rocks. She hadn't failed to surprise him, yet. Henry, however, was another matter. The boy hadn't spoken a single word to him at all. It was something he vowed to remedy.

He looked over at the horse, Captain, if he remembered the name right. It stood at the side of the road, licking the bark of a tall oak. Thirst could make an animal do strange things. Most people assumed that bigger horses had more reserves, so they could handle

55

thirst and hunger better. But, that was the exact opposite of the truth. Large horses required more to keep them going.

He eyed the horse speculatively, noting the hanging head and drooping ears as it ceased its ministrations to the tree and just stood there. It had even refused the handful of oats Fiera had offered it earlier. The animal was in bad shape. He needed water now, not sometime tomorrow from a merchant that may or may not exist.

Turning back to Fiera, who was intent upon a stone she hefted to feel its weight, Efar made a circle motion with his hand. "I'm going to check around. See where our nearest neighbors are and try to find out if there are any robbers lurking about."

She didn't even look at him, merely nodded and waved her hand, her attention returning to the ground at her feet as the rock in her hand disappeared into her pocket. The dust cloud began again. Very odd girl, indeed.

Efar slipped into the skeleton forest on the western side of the road, opposite the direction Henry had taken. Once he found a thick copse of close-knit, though bare, shrubs, he stopped. Looking around, Efar decided he was alone. Though nakedness was a way of life for shifters, people who weren't used to it often had problems. He undressed and reached for the griffin. Immediately, a deep ache slowly pulsed in his bones throughout his whole body. His chest widened and deepened, pushing his thickening arms toward the ground. His shoulder blades became heavy with gigantic wings. His face stretched into an eagle's beak and eyes. From his waist down, he changed into a lion, keeping it slow, so it didn't hurt. The whole process took the rest of the daylight and dusk to complete. Change finished, he glanced about for bystanders one more time and then

56

launched into the darkening night, heading straight north as fast as he could. This trip of his had never had anything to do with neighbors or robbers, as he'd told Fiera. It was all about that horse and the water it so desperately needed. He had to get to the merchant before the cart reached the safety of the city. Otherwise, he'd have to raid within the confines of the city walls, against hundreds of armed men.

Below his outstretched wings, the forest magically filled out with leaves the more north he sped. Nocturnal animals made their debut. He didn't realize how much he'd missed the green living woods. How could anyone live for a prolonged time in a sterile area like the one behind him?

After almost forty-five minutes of flying, he saw the massive walls of a large city in the distance, bright within from candle-lit lamps and bold orange street fires. As he closed on it, he spied the merchant cart, water jugs of every shape on its roof, trundling toward the city gates and the stream of people waiting to enter, three armed guards riding alongside. It was only about two hundred yards out from the bridge over the River Dee, immediately in front of the gates. But, it was still too far for the city guards to assist. Though, that would change rapidly if he didn't get moving. He folded his wings back and dove like an arrow.

Neither the guards, nor the merchant, expected an attack from above. Efar landed on the wagon, rocking it heavily with the impact of his weight. Most of the smaller jugs were empty, but two large ones near the driver were still full. Before any of the men could understand what they saw, Efar wrapped his giant eagle claws around the handles of the two jugs and snatched them off the cart. Climbing again into the sky with his trophies, he thought he just might get away with his robbery.

He was slower than he anticipated, however, with the weight of the water. The guards at last loosed their bows, and arrows hurtled toward him. Most missed. One pierced the vessel in his left claw, shattering it. Water and shards rained down on the soldiers. Another arrow struck home, lodging in the meaty part of his left lion's thigh. The pain of it seared through him, even as he flew out of range.

He'd gone straight up, facing west, to mislead anyone who might think to search for griffins. This protected his home and family far to the southeast. Once out of sight, hissing from the pain of the arrow point stuck in his leg, he juggled the water vessel to hold it in both claws so as to not unbalance himself. He curved to the south. It took longer to return, due to the extra weight. By the time he reached his destination, it was a good two hours since he'd told Fiera he was leaving. Clouds that had been on the edge of the night sky were now scattered across it.

He landed awkwardly, holding the earthen water jug tight against his chest to protect it. He let his one good lion's leg take the brunt of the impact, but he couldn't help putting some weight on his injured leg, stumbling and hissing again through his griffin's beak. Setting down the jug, he lifted his wing and turned to inspect his wound. The shaft of the arrow stuck out at a downward angle from his bloodstained lion's fur, but the head was buried deep in bulging muscle. A steady stream of blood ran down his leg.

From the left, leaves shuffled lightly and he snapped his attention toward the sound. There stood Henry, staring, not at him, but at the arrow fixed in his leg. The boy glanced at him, meeting his gaze frankly and gestured toward the arrow. Efar nodded. He could only assume the child knew who he was and understood the arrow had to be removed before he changed back to human form. If not taken out, the damage would be catastrophic.

Henry approached, all hesitancy gone. He dipped under Efar's outstretched wing and gripped the feathered shaft with both hands. The boy pulled, but the arrowhead stayed firmly imbedded. He carefully placed one foot on the griffin's big leg, leaned back and pulled with everything he had. Sweat broke out on his face.

Efar's vision swam. The searing pain made him understand the arrow had sunk all the way into the bone. He clacked his beak and snaked his neck back and forth. The only thing the griffin wanted was to make the pain stop. Somewhere in his animal brain, he reasoned the boy was the cause. Efar fought his instincts with all the strength of his will to overcome the drive to attack the child beneath his wing.

Then suddenly the arrow broke free. The boy flew backwards, sprawling on the forest floor. Efar sank to the ground, face down, letting the animal hide within him once again and the human reemerge. Lifting his head to inspect his wound, he saw that the gash had remained the size of the arrowhead. That was good, but the blood that coated his leg from thigh to foot worried him. He'd lost a lot.

Henry scrambled over to him and pushed a wad of leaves against the injury. With his other hand, he fumbled in a hidden pouch at the waistband of his trousers. He pulled out a packet. In one smooth movement, he removed the leaves with one hand and poured the contents of the packet into the wound with the other. Then he replaced the leaves.

It felt like a burning hot coal had been wedged into Efar's leg. He moaned, closing his eyes. The griffin once again welled up within him, trying to break free. Then, as suddenly as it began, the pain ceased, leaving him shaking and weak as a newborn.

****

Fiera stirred the campfire. Sparks shot into the night sky like seedpods seeking a new home. Like her. Like them all. Even Efar, who claimed to be just traveling, seemed to be looking for...something missing from his life, something to rest in.

Leaves crunched and sticks popped across the road. Startled, Fiera jerked her head up, ready to run. To her surprise, Efar limped from behind a thick stand of dried up spruces and bare-branched shrubs, leaning heavily on Marie's shoulder, blood oozing down his pants leg.

Fiera sprang to her feet and raced to support Efar's other side. "What happened?"

"We have water for Captain. There, in the woods behind us." He jerked his head toward his left shoulder.

Instinctively, she glanced in the direction he'd indicated, but saw nothing. Returning her attention to him, she asked again, "What happened to you? Where'd you get the water?"

He gave a grimace. "Well, after I told you I don't steal, I stole it."

They reached the road and hobbled silently across it. It wasn't until after they carefully lowered Efar to the ground by the fire and he situated himself with his leg outstretched that she spoke again. She crossed her arms and stood in front of him, Marie beside her. "Tell me how you got injured."

He glanced at Marie and nodded. Then, he dropped his gaze and began fussing with the position of his leg. Not looking up, he said, "As it happens, I'm a griffin."

With his admission, Marie tapped Fiera's arm. She cupped her hands like a bowl. Fiera nodded absently. Efar was a griffin. She'd heard of those, but they were just myth, weren't they? Taking up the rope bridle that was really the lard-thickened blanket, she turned her back on the wounded man and fashioned a wide and deep bowl with her magic.

Snatching the container from her hands, Marie ran into the forest.

Fiera called to Captain in her mind. *Follow Marie. She has water for you. Don't drink too much, too fast, or you'll get a belly ache.*

I'll be careful, he promised. The horse jogged after the girl like a puppy after its master.

Turning back to Efar, Fiera saw that he was staring after the two, his mouth wide open. She said, "That doesn't explain how you got injured."

He jerked his gaze to her and frowned. "Why doesn't your brother like me? He doctored me," he motioned toward his leg with both hands, "but he won't talk to me."

"Answer my question." She shoved her foot against his bloody leg, satisfied to see him wince as the message drove home.

"I saw how bad off your horse was. So, after I told you I was checking out the area, I instead shifted to griffin and flew ahead to find water. Spotting your merchant, I dove in and stole a couple large vessels of water. The merchant's guards shot me with an arrow and destroyed one of the jugs as I flew away. When I landed back here, Henry saw me and doctored my injury. End of story. Your turn. Why doesn't he like me?"

"Show me."

"That I'm a griffin? Now? I'm injured!"

She shrugged. She had no doubt he was telling the truth, but she needed to see his honesty with her own two eyes. Especially if she was going to reveal her own secrets.

"You are a very stubborn girl." He rubbed his

61

temples. "Fine. Will part of me suffice? I don't want to aggravate my injury more."

At her single quick nod, he dramatically pulled his shirt off over his head. The firelight danced across his skin, getting lost in the rows of muscles below his solid chest. His neatly corded upper arms were bigger than her leg. "It hurts more if I go fast, so be patient."

Fiera settled on the ground and stared unblinkingly at him. She didn't want to miss a thing. After a few moments, she noticed his chest seemed to be growing. The thick rolls of muscles lengthened to wrap around his sides. Nubs from his back showed above his shoulders, and his nose seemed to be bigger. His wrists thickened and his fingers elongated.

A fine down sprouted across all his skin, even as his nose hooked at the tip into a beak. His fingernails slowly became long dagger-sharp talons. The nubs on his shoulders grew pointed and Fiera stared at them for a few moments before she realized with a start that they were the beginnings of wings.

She pursed her lips. How many times had she wished for wings, eager to escape the confines of her prison-like home? Her life would have been so different. She wouldn't have been forced to live in shame for being a witch. It became her parents' legacy to her, that shame.

As Efar's face became more bird-like, his wings stretched to two feet in length. Then four. Then seven. The down on his body aged into feathers.

Fiera scrambled to her feet again and slowly approached what was now a birdman: bird on top, man on bottom. With only a cursory glance at his bright bird eyes, she reached out her hand and lightly traced her finger the length of one wing, parting her lips, suddenly unable to get enough air. What it must be like to soar above the mundane!

She walked behind him, noting the thickness of the wing hinge. Placing a hand on either side, she tried to measure it. Each attachment was easily as wide as her waist.

Firelight bounced and flickered across the flat smoothness of the griffin's feathers. She stroked her fingers down the length of them: the straight feather shaft, the silky vane, and the strong razor-like edge. She spoke for the first time since Efar had begun his transformation. "They're so beautiful."

Crossing around the tip of the wing, she returned to the front. He glanced at her with his eagle eyes and then looked away, as if embarrassed. It suddenly occurred to her how forward she'd been, touching him. Investigating his body. The heat of a blush burned in her cheeks. "I...I'm sorry. I didn't mean..." She closed her eyes and took a deep breath, hoping for the color to leave her face. Opening them again, she said, "Thank you."

Captain's voice exploded into her mind. *I knew it! He's not normal! He's a monster!*

She spun around to find the horse blowing hard, his nostrils flared wide, eyes wild, and his legs in a constant dance, moving him forward and back, from side to side.

In a flash of ingenuity, Marie had tied the water jug to his tail, letting him carry half the weight. As he shifted back and forth in fear, she doggedly moved with him, holding tightly to the other handle to keep the water from spilling.

Fiera rushed to the horse. *Captain! Stop! Hold still!*

The horse appeared not to have even heard her. He continued rocking left and right, wanting to attack, yet afraid to come close to the winged beast.

Stop! She wrapped her arms around her mount's

63

massive neck. He stopped moving, but beneath his skin, she felt him trembling.

By the time Marie had the jug untied, Efar had shifted completely back to human and had managed to stand. He walked slowly toward the horse, shirt still off, his hand outstretched in a gesture of friendship.

That's all it took. Captain laid his ears flat back against his head and lunged at the man, snapping violently with his big yellow teeth. *I'll protect us! I'll kill that monster!*

Fiera, who still clung to the horse's neck, was dragged with him. She shouted at Efar, "Get back! Can't you see how frightened he is? What's wrong with you?"

Efar opened his eyes wide and stumbled backwards, nearly tripping on their small pile of supplies.

She called Marie. "Come get Captain. Take him somewhere and see if you can calm him down."

She tore off a piece of her shirt, pushed her magic into it and fashioned another bridle. Hanging it on the horse's head, she said, *Captain, this man is not our enemy, no matter what manner of creature he hides. Go with Marie. Have some oats. I'll get things sorted.*

Still blowing through his flared nostrils, Captain let Marie lead him away, though he danced sideways so as to keep an eye on his new nemesis. *Don't trust him!*

Fiera watched the duo walk down the road long enough to ensure they were going to be all right. With a sigh, she turned back to the man by the fire.

Chapter 5

Bartheleme landed in dragon form next to his father's agent. The clouds obscuring the moon didn't matter much for his shifter vision, but the fat agent he'd requested seemed to have trouble seeing exactly what was swooping down on him. The man stumbled backward with a gasp of surprise, even though he'd been told of the massive size of this dragon.

Shifting to human form, Bartheleme took the clothing the other man offered from a trembling hand. By the time he'd dressed, the agent had control of his emotions once more and swept into a low bow. Bartheleme said, "Rise. Do you have any news?"

Together, they walked toward the requested horses. The fat man shook his head. "My Prince, I had one, at a little burg called Midden, but she disappeared. I feel certain she was spirited away by another I strongly suspect as also witch. I followed their trail, even found where they'd camped for the night. However, the myriad of tracks at a large crossroads made it impossible to tell which way they'd gone."

Bartheleme stopped and faced the man. "Why do

65

you think the first was a witch? What indicators did she give?"

The fat agent blushed, no doubt thinking that his judgment was being questioned. "It was a subtle case, Your Majesty. The inhabitants of Midden did not die from the famine. True, some moved away, but every one of them lived. I know of no other village in England unaffected thusly. Furthermore, they seemed to possess an uncanny strength. There was a mute child assisting in the kitchen at the time."

Nodding in agreement at the man's assessment, Bartheleme continued toward the waiting mounts. Often parents cut out the tongue of a suspected witch child, keeping it from casting spells. They hoped to keep the child safe that way. "And the second one?"

"She was near death, riding on a giant of a horse. She had this." He held out a gold coin. "Where did a girl, starving as she was, get these things?"

"She could have stolen them." Bartheleme shrugged and took the offered coin. He hefted it, feeling the unnatural weight of it. He bit into it, but it refused to dent. Surprised, he raised his eyebrows at the agent.

The fat man gave a knowing smile. "We tried cutting it with a cleaver, but it wouldn't split. Sire," he leaned in close, "her eyes were green."

"What did she say? How did she explain these things?" They'd reached the horses, and Bartheleme stroked the neck of a handsome chestnut mare. She showed no skittishness at his dragon smell. Nor did the white-flecked black beside her. They'd both been raised in one of his family's holdings.

"She said not a word. No one had seen her before, either. Yet, she seemed to know about the other witch in the kitchen."

Bartheleme felt his pulse quicken. Could it be they'd finally found what his father had been searching

66

for: a mind-speaker? "You said you lost them at the crossroads, is that right?"

"It is, Sire. My apologies. I followed one branch to here, being pressed for our meeting time, but I found no trace of them. I would have thought they'd avoid large cities, but my guess now is they went to Chester."

Bartheleme mounted. "Then, we too shall go to Chester."

****

A fat raindrop fell from the sky onto Fiera's arm. She looked up at the overcast night, still able to see stars through the clouds' grip. She doubted it would even turn into a real shower. Probably just a few drops here and there. No help for anyone.

Efar had returned to his outstretched position by the fire, blood seeping from the wound. Even in pain, his eyes danced in merriment. Fiera squatted beside him, motioning to his injury. "Press your hand against it so it'll form a scab."

He pushed the heel of his left hand against his leg and looked up at her, contrite. "I'm really sorry about the horse."

She pressed her lips together and gave a quick nod. The man had no common sense when it came to animals. Twice, he'd tried to touch a spooked horse. She'd have to teach him about the nature of real creatures, specifically Captain, if he was going to continue to travel with them. But first, she'd promised him an answer. "Marie can't talk to you. Someone cut out her tongue."

"Marie? A sister, not a brother."

Fiera stood and shook her head. "We're not family."

Efar sucked in a breath and comprehension lit his eyes. "You stole her from the inn in Midden! That's why the fat man is hunting for you. I thought it might be because of the horse, or even your hair. You two look like Danes. But it was her. Why is she so important?"

She dropped her gaze to her hands in her lap. She had to tell him now or she never would. Since a young age, she'd been taught to never tell anyone about her true nature. But, she was finished with that now. True, she may need to camouflage herself from time to time, like now, but she would no longer deny her true self.

Taking a deep breath to calm her rolling stomach, she reached into her pocket, pulled out one of her gathered stones, and showed it to him. Then she closed her hand and concentrated, willing her magic to change the rock. When she opened her hand again, a shiny gold coin sat there. "We're witches."

Efar kept his gaze on the coin, but his mouth slowly dropped open. He reached into her hand, took the gold coin, and held it near the fire, studying it. "Witches."

She removed her cap and ran her hand over her hair, turning it to its normal fawn red. "This is my normal color."

Staring at her, still holding the coin, he said, "You were brown-headed in Midden. Red hair means nothing where I come from. It's common enough. Though, coupled with those green eyes..."

He frowned and glanced back at the coin. "So you didn't need me to get water, after all."

"We did." She explained about her abilities and limitations, adding the part of speaking to animals last.

"Can you speak to my griffin?"

She shook her head slowly, pressing her lips into a thin line. "I don't know. It's not really an animal."

"As soon as I'm comfortable enough, I'll change all the way and we'll try it." He paused and then motioned toward Captain as the horse and Marie reappeared within the ring of the fire's glow. "What does he say about me?"

Captain's voice echoed in her head. *I don't like him. Not that anyone listens.*

She ignored him and said to Efar, "I think that's pretty obvious."

"I suppose it is." He continued to watch as Marie brushed the horse. "She's a healer?"

"Potions."

"That black horse the man from Midden was riding is from a dragon holding, I'm pretty sure."

"Captain said he stunk."

Efar barked a laugh. "I suppose all us shifters do to a real animal."

Captain again butted into Fiera's mind. *Yes they do! They stink all the way to heaven! He's ruining my nose!*

Oblivious to the horse's diatribe in Fiera's head, Efar continued. "There have been rumors the dragons have been searching for something or someone. Now we know it's witches. They've obviously joined with King Æthelred. We just don't know why."

"We?"

"Us shifters. More specifically, the griffins."

"We had werewolves where I grew up. Or at least rumors of them. I never saw any."

Captain interrupted. *They stink, too.*

He risked his life to get water for you.

Stinky water. He tainted it. I think --

I think Efar is lucky not to have to listen to you.

You're taking his side?

Fiera said the only thing that would shut the horse up. *I am, for now.*

Efar apparently hadn't noticed her distraction. "—werewolves are real. For any animal, there's usually a shifter animal."

69

She nodded as if she'd heard the whole explanation. She'd said she was taking his side. She'd even told him her secret because he'd told his and she wanted to remain on equal footing with him. A griffin would have an edge over a normal human, but not necessarily a witch. At least that's the reason she told herself. But did she really trust him?

****

Wide awake, Efar stared into the unfurling smoke of the fire, trying to calm his clamoring heart. Fiera and Marie were witches! And they hadn't been scared of the griffin at all. They'd actually seemed more afraid of him finding out about them. In the time of church-sanctioned purgings, there were scarier things for a witch than shapeshifters.

After a dinner of cheese and rock hard bread, soup for Fiera, Marie had bedded down for the night on the other side of the fire. But Fiera was brushing Captain. Occasionally, she paused and looked deep into the horse's eyes. Once, she shook her head violently. The horse flicked his ears back at that, swinging his head to glare at Efar. If a horse could glare.

Efar studied Fiera during the silent conversation. She was going to make quite a woman when she grew up. The boy's clothing curved gently around hips that flared a bit too wide for a boy. When she'd taken her cap off earlier to show him her hair, the gauntness of her face hadn't hidden the beauty that would bloom as she aged.

His skin still felt the way she'd run her finger along the top of his wing. And that voice! He figured her to be between thirteen and fifteen. Sixteen at the outside. Too young for him. There was a time in his life, even recently, that he might have pursued her, but even though "old enough to wed is old enough to bed" was common practice in that day, it wasn't good enough for him anymore. With a heavy sigh, he turned away.

Fiera left the horse, checked on Marie, and then came and settled near him. "Captain has offered to stand guard tonight. He says he'll watch out for all manner of evil, including flying ones." She didn't smile, but her eyes did.

He called to the horse. "Captain! My thanks. Even evil flying creatures need a good night's sleep."

For answer, Captain laid his ears back and turned his hips to them.

Efar laughed out loud, mirth filling his belly.

Fiera smiled then and it lit up her whole face with an unexpected softness, rounding out the harsh starvation lines. The girl was stunning, even as thin as she was and in her youth. Efar caught his breath and it took a moment before he jerked his stare away.

"What?"

He heard the sudden frown in her voice, so he faced her again and gave his best grin. "That's the first time I've seen you smile."

"I've had very little to smile about in my life."

"We'll have to change that. You're beautiful when you smile."

A slow rose-colored bloom crept from her neck all the way to her temples. She ducked her head with a shy droop of her sweeping eyelashes. His lion's sense of smell picked up a gentle blush of her pheromones as they filled the air around them in a soft cloud. With a start, Efar realized that she was no child. Before he realized what he was doing, he reached out his hand and brushed the back of his fingers against her heated cheek. "How old are you?"

She pulled back and stared at him, a heavy frown on her face and fear clear in her olive eyes. She didn't

71

leave, though.

Efar dropped his hand, silently cursing himself at his callousness. For a moment the only sound was the snap and hiss of the fire.

Then, in her low, smooth voice, she said, "I'm nineteen."

Nineteen! Fiera was a full-grown woman! It was obvious by her reaction to his caress, however, that she didn't have much experience with men. Or maybe she did, but subscribed to the church morality and wasn't interested in a tryst. "Earlier today, when I asked where you're from, you seemed sad. What happened to you?"

"Some witches hide easier than others. Because of my hair and eyes, my parents realized my identity when I was an early age. From that moment on, I wasn't allowed outside the house. To most of the people of our village, I'd died."

Efar sucked in his breath. He couldn't imagine a life like that. No one to understand her and a prisoner in her own home. His heart ached for her pain. "You ran away."

She managed a fleeting smile. "That would have been better. Actually, they died a few days ago from the famine."

"I'm sorry." The words felt so inadequate to him.

"Lots of people have died." Shrugging, Fiera half turned away and wiped her eyes. She motioned to his leg. "How is it?"

Glad for the change of topic, his words came in a rush. "Good. I mean it hurts, but not as much. I should be ready to travel tomorrow."

"You'll ride and I'll walk."

"Do you really believe he'll let me onboard?" Efar chuckled and motioned to the giant horse dozing on his feet, left hip cocked. "I'll be fine walking. It'll keep me from getting too stiff."

They stared at the fire in mutual silence. Efar leaned back, soaking in the sweetness of their budding friendship. Fiera had a faraway look in her eyes and seemed lost in her thoughts. He wished those thoughts were about him, but he didn't think they were. No doubt her mind was filled with memories of her parents. He wanted to hold her, to comfort her, but she'd turn him away, no doubt. Still, the fact that she stayed at the fire, close to him, meant his presence soothed her somehow.

On the other side of the fire, the shadow that was Captain lifted its head and stared off into the skeleton trees. The horse startled and shied toward them as a rope sailed neatly from behind a large dead spruce.

Efar sprang to his feet and bolted toward Captain, ignoring the slice of pain in his leg. He turned to yell for Fiera, but found her beside him. "Get Marie!" Even as she stopped and veered toward the sleeping girl, he was reaching deep inside for the griffin.

****

"Wake up!" Fiera shook Marie. She'd never known someone to sleep so deeply. It was as if the child was dead. Two shadows appeared from behind a thick copse of dried-up pine shrubs.

She shook the girl with more violence, nearly jerking her off the ground. Finally, she was rewarded by the opening of one groggy eye. Fiera pointed at the approaching men. "Robbers!"

Marie followed her point and, when her gaze lit on the menacing figures, she let out an inarticulate cry and scrambled to her feet.

Fiera turned to run, tugging on the girl's arm to follow, but Marie jerked free and pulled a packet out of her pouch. Opening it flat, she faced the two men and blew a fine white powder into their faces.

With shrieks and howls, the highwaymen pawed at boils that magically spread on their skin. The closer thief dropped to his knees immediately, his face blanketed with watery pustules. His friend, who had been a bit behind the first, managed to get his face nearly covered in time and only a few boils bubbled up on his brow and cheeks. The backs of his hands, however, were a mass of blisters. In a roar of anger, puffs of torn clothing flying in the air, his body instantly shifted to that of nightmares: the werewolf!

Open-mouthed, Fiera stared. Coarse black hair coated it from head to toe and it had a long thick snout peopled with sharp teeth that snicked into place. Arms extended to below its knees. Its paws were still covered in the awful blisters, but sharp claws curved from its fingers.

Marie gasped and stumbled backward into Fiera.

The beast growled and advanced.

Grabbing Marie's hand again, Fiera turned and ran. Neither of them were a match for the monster at their heels. They ran toward where a griffin soared above three men who had surrounded Captain. A rope lay on the big horse's shoulders, its one loose end dangling on the far side and its other end firmly wound around the hand of a robber. Captain reared, striking out with his front feet at the nearest highwayman and the rope slid to the ground.

Efar folded his wings and dove for one of the men. The thief saw him coming, but wasn't quick enough to evade the talons that pierced his shoulder, lifted him into the air, and then tossed him against the trunk of a leafless stout oak.

The beast behind Fiera and Marie was closing ground. "Efar!"

At the sound of his name, the griffin lifted his head. In that split second, the werewolf swiped at Marie, spinning her around and raking its giant claws across her tiny body. The violence of the action pulled the child's hand out of Fiera's grasp and flung her across the road where she fell like a limp rag.

"Marie!" Fiera's breath caught in her throat, nearly choking her and she ran toward the fallen girl, the werewolf right behind. As she crumpled to the cracked earth beside her young friend, she heard the sound of something big and heavy hitting a wall. Or, more correctly, a wall hitting something big and heavy. Turning, she saw that Efar had flown right into the werewolf, knocking it from its path of attack. The force of the impact threw them both end-for-end across the hard-packed earth into the bank of skeleton trees.

Fiera leaned over Marie, listening. After a beat, she heard a soft, slow inhale. The child was alive! Barely. She scooped up the injured girl and cradled her in her lap.

Marie's shirt hung in ribbons across her body. Fiera pulled it off and used it to blot the cuts on the child's chest. The injuries were deep, but her ribs had stopped the claws from reaching her inner organs— though two of her ribs felt like they might have been broken.

Captain was gone, as were the two remaining men who'd been trying to catch him. The robber they'd fought by the fire was still there, but he wasn't going anywhere, blinded by blisters as he was.

Efar and the werewolf fought among the tree trunks across the road. They dodged skull-breaking swings of heavy arms or club-like wings. The dark monster swiped at the griffin with the same claws that injured Marie, missing by breaths of an inch. Efar snaked his hooked beak at the beast, grabbing its thick arm before it could begin its backswing. Then the griffin raised its eagle talon, placed it on the side of the monster's face, and pushed. They stood that way as if frozen in time. Then, with a loud snap, and the werewolf dropped to the ground with a broken neck.

The griffin turned and walked to Fiera, lowered his front end, and spread his closest wing into a ramp. The message was clear: they were going to fly.

Holding Marie tightly against her, Fiera walked up the wing, stepping as lightly as she could. The moment she settled, Efar took two long strides and pushed off into the air, nearly unseating her again. His mighty wings beat in rhythm, pulling air beneath them, lifting them higher, the muscles flexing beneath Fiera's legs.

The ground shrank below them and the bare trees sped past. Cool night air blew against her and she changed the bloody rags into a blanket, wrapping it around Marie and crushing her close to keep her warm. There was nothing more she could do for her young friend. Now, it would be up to a doctor. She whispered in Marie's ear. "Hang on!"

The forest beneath them began to darken and the smell of green growing things filled the dry air. The forest was alive! She peered out at the shapeless masses of trees, wishing for daylight so she could see the beauty of what lay below.

A glow appeared on the horizon and, for a brief moment, she thought her wish had been granted, but then she realized it was lights from the city. Leaning over Marie again, she said, "We're almost there. I can see it."

****

Efar landed in a tiny forest glade near the brightly-lit Chester bridge. Merchant tents littered the sides of the road and, even at that late hour, travelers streamed into the city. Small boats, offloaded from large merchant ships at the mouth of the river, crowded the shore, riding low in the depleted water, filled with heaps of goods.

As soon as Fiera dismounted with Marie, he shifted to his man form. He pointed at the four guards on either side of the gate. "You take her and run as fast as you can across the bridge to those men. Tell them you were attacked and your daughter needs a doctor. You have to remember she's your daughter or they might not act as quickly. Do you understand?"

Fiera nodded, her face pale, her olive eyes dark.

"Good. I'll go find Captain." He let his gaze rove over her face for a moment and then cupped her cheek in his hand. Leaning in, he kissed her gently. Her lips tasted like rose petals floating in fine wine and they were as soft as silk. Regret thickened his voice. "Darken your hair. Change your clothes back into a dress. Run like the wind." He gave her a gentle push toward the bridge.

She turned and ran, weaving through the trees, her hair turning brown as she went. He watched her race past patrons across the lit bridge, pants becoming dress, screaming for help, until she reached the guards. One of them appropriated a traveler's steed, mounted with Marie, and charged into the city, Fiera running at his heels.

Efar let out his breath in a rush, aware he'd been holding it for too long. Marie would be all right. She had to be. Now, to find Captain. Turning, he shifted griffin in three strides and took to the night sky, heading south again.

It pleased him Fiera hadn't made a fuss about his nakedness. She seemed to take it in stride as a practical necessity. As she had the kiss. Yet...

He frowned. Why would she accept his kiss now,

when she'd rejected his earlier caress? It didn't make sense. He tried to clear his mind, to float thoughtless on the night breeze, but he kept returning to the kiss. It had lit him up from the inside. He'd never felt anything like it, not even with Gabriella. It wasn't just passion. There had also been a desire to secure Fiera as his. As if he'd been in love. He'd experienced that plenty before, but never so soon after meeting a woman. It felt different a bit, almost as if they were supposed to be together, as if they already belonged to each other. What did it mean?

Reaching their campsite after flying hard for another half hour, Efar landed and took a quick look around. The man injured by the fire was gone, but the dead werewolf was still dead. As was the man he'd thrown against the tree.

He studied the road edge near where Captain had been fighting. On the west side of the road was nothing, but on the east were hoof prints heading into the dried out forest. Boot prints followed. Some were scuffed, as if they'd been dragged a fair bit. Good boy, Captain!

Efar checked his wound. The scab had finally broken and blood oozed down his leg. No time for that now. He had to find the horse.

Excellent in the daylight, his eagle eyesight wasn't well suited for night flying. But, as long as the trees had no leaves, he should be able see well enough. Lunging into the sky again, Efar slowly headed east, overlooking the sharp stakes of the trees, following Captain's trail. The horse and his captors were at least two hours ahead of him, still. He put every ounce of energy he had into the pursuit. He should be able to catch them; they were, after all, on foot and working with a temperamental horse. As he feared, though, the trail arced toward the green, past the northern edge of the drought zone. Within moments, the canopy of leaves was too dense for Efar to see through.

He landed and shifted to man, letting the griffin sleep, and cursing his lack of clothes in the thickness of the night. Boots, at least, would have been nice.

Though it was darker beneath the sprawling branches, heavy with leaves, the trail was nearly as clear to him as it had been from above, before the trees had blocked it from sight. The trail was wide, with broken saplings and branches. Deep gouges marred the loose loam where Captain had dug in his hooves and fought his captors. Efar followed this trail for more than an hour, sure he was gaining ground.

Then, as he crossed a horizontal wide rock face, still sun-warm beneath his feet, all signs of Captain's passing suddenly disappeared!

Thinking that the thieves had turned while on the rock slab, he walked the edges of the monumental shelf, searching for the exit path. He found none.

He returned to where the trail led onto the rock and checked that the thieves hadn't backtracked on the same prints. But, no. Every hoofmark and boot print was heading onto the rock.

Efar turned round and round. Moonlight shone on the stone, turning it nearly luminescent and highlighting crisscrossing cracks, some filled with blown dirt and the occasional sprouting seed. There were no hoofmarks or prints of any kind. Nor were there any scuffs of freshly chipped rock. It was as if Captain had been spirited away!

Standing with his hands on his hips and tapping the horizontal stone shelf with his bare foot, Efar considered how a horse could just disappear. He let his gaze rove the breadth of the rock slab and slowly raised his head to view the window of night sky above. A large flying creature—say, a dragon—could have landed here, snatched up Captain, and flown away. And he, Efar, wouldn't have seen it because he was *below* the canopy of trees, following on foot.

Without hesitation, he shifted to griffin, clenching his jaw at the icy pain that scored his bones and muscles, and launched into the furious dark between midnight and dawn, after what he believed to be ahead of him but couldn't yet see. He drove his wings hard, tucking his lion's feet and eagle's claws tightly against his body, cramping his injured leg, in an effort to streamline his flight.

The dragon had to be big to carry a horse like Captain. It didn't matter though. No dragon could out fly a griffin. And Efar was the fastest in all the griffin family. He'd proven it many, many times.

The thieves were currently headed north, but they'd have to turn west sometime, toward the dragon holdings on the edge of their territories. Worried they might have already turned, Efar kept a constant scan to both the north and the west.

The dragon was on the furthest edge of his vision, straight ahead, to the north; he hadn't turned yet. It was flying just below the grey puffs of scattered clouds. As he gained on it, he saw it was a giant of a beast, yet it labored heavily, swinging the horse like a pendulum beneath it. Captain didn't help by squirming. The horse probably didn't realize that, if he got loose, he'd fall to his death. Serious injury, anyway.

There was a single rider atop the dragon. So, Efar thought, a dragon hadn't landed; one of the thieves was a shapeshifter. Was the other?

****

The chair Fiera sat in was hard and she'd been in it for hours. Squirming, she tried to find a place on her bottom that wasn't sore from the unyielding wood. The moans of those sick and dying surrounded her. She hunched further into the corner of the temporary cloth walls, glancing around to see if anyone was watching.

Marie laid beside her, a small lump that didn't even stretch the full length of the bed. White salve lay thick in the cuts made by the werewolf. The scent of lavender water was heavy about her. She lay so still and was so pale that Fiera watched closely to see that her young friend still breathed.

They should have listened to Efar and taken the eastern road. So far their...her...stubbornness had gotten one person injured, one nearly dead, and one missing. She'd had the foresight to remove Marie's potion pouch, but with nowhere to hide it, had tied it around her own waist. If it were found, everyone would know she and Marie were witches.

Fiera shifted on the chair again so that her weight was only on one side of her bottom. Sitting and waiting had never been her strong point. She sighed. If only someone was there to speak with, Efar or even Captain.

Thinking of Efar brought up the memory of his kiss. She'd been too worried about Marie at the time to really comprehend the significance of it. She'd barely noticed he'd done it. She touched her fingers to her lips, remembering the firm heat of his mouth on hers and the passionate depths in his eyes. Her heart swelled so that she found herself breathing hard. Her stomach felt like it had butterflies in it. She closed her eyes and tried to recapture the spice of his male scent next to her.

Abruptly, she threw her eyes open, her whole body heated in a furious blush. There was something besides the kiss she hadn't noticed in her concern over Marie: Efar had been naked! She turned her face toward the wall and squinched her eyes shut tight.

Her mind refused to obey her commands to not see Efar. Her memory traveled over every inch of his body, every pore, every—

Fiera jumped to her feet and began pacing. *Stop! Stop! Stop!* She pounded her fists against her thighs and ground her teeth. All her life she'd only had contact with one man, her father, and he'd kept himself decently covered. Even when he and her mother had sex in the large bed across the room from hers, they'd done it under the blankets.

She'd been taught what the church preached. Nakedness and sex were done only in the privacy of marriage. Now, the first man she met not only kissed her, but he'd shown her his full body!

True, he'd just come from being a griffin and returned right back to one, so he had an excuse. A good one, at that. But, he'd kissed her *while* naked! In the eyes of the church, that had to be tantamount to falling into Hell itself. The fact that she couldn't banish the image from her mind twice condemned her.

She sank to the chair again, with a moan. Thrice condemned because she was a witch.

The clip of shoes on stone brought her attention to a small, stocky man rapidly approaching. Her senses tingled, sharpening into a narrow focus on him. This man was a witch.

He stopped at Marie's bedside with a frown. He barely noticed the injured girl; all his attention was on Fiera. He spoke in a low voice, laced with urgency. "We must get you out of the public eye. There are many in this city that seek to destroy our kind."

Fiera stood and gestured to Marie, angry that he assumed she'd abandon her friend. "I'm not leaving her behind."

He shook his head, frowning harder. "Nor will you have to. She's also one of us. We care for our own." He peered over his shoulder and at all points in the giant room. He even left the bedside and checked behind every cloth partition, of which there were quite a few.

Seemingly satisfied, he returned and slid his arms beneath Marie, lifting her. Without a second look back, he turned and strode straight for the exit. Fiera hurried after him. For such a short man, he moved quickly; she had to half-run just to keep up.

The main door led them directly onto the drive that approached and then circled the Abbey. In the dark of post-midnight, they followed straight down the cobblestone drive and turned toward the east gate once they came to the road. Before they reached it, however, they turned south again, on a road that eventually curved to run along the city wall. At the first crossroad, a thinly trampled path, they turned west, passing a dark dwelling on the left before stopping at the next. This house was brightly lit and, when the door opened to the man's gentle kick, light spilled onto the street from the owner's candle. The woman was as a scarecrow, very tall and lean. Behind her, several more people appeared holding candles. She reached her arm around the short man and propelled him inside. "Hurry, Laurence! Before someone sees you three!" Looking over the top of his head at Fiera, she said, "I'm Gwen. This is my house. You're safe here."

Fiera and Laurence, still carrying Marie, were ushered down a long hallway into a large kitchen. There the woman paused and leaned low over the injured girl, examining the wounds. "These are deep. If we don't do something now, she won't survive the dawn. What's her name?"

Fiera's breath caught. The monks at the abbey hadn't told her the injuries were that bad. Tears sprang to her eyes and spilled down her cheeks. Her friend could die! "She can't talk, but she likes it when I call her Marie."

Gwen, freakishly tall, nodded and led them out the back door to a barn behind. The people in the house hadn't been all of those present. Three more people in long gowns swept the straw from the dirt floor at the center of the barn. As they swept, a pattern of inset stones became apparent: a large star pointing north in the center of an even larger circle.

Laurence laid Marie in the center of the star, her head aligned with the tip, at the north.

Gwen came close to Fiera, bending from the waist to peer in her face. "What did this to her?"

"A werewolf."

The group in the barn hushed and then softly began to whisper. The tall woman straightened and, one by one, they quieted. She returned her attention to Fiera, but didn't bend to look in her face again. "A werewolf? Are you sure?"

"I saw it change."

Gwen pressed her lips close together, nodded, and turned to her group again. "Let's prepare."

The candles were blown out, all except for Laurence's. He took Fiera's arm and gently piloted her toward the door of the barn. "You can't stay."

"What will they do to her?" She looked back over her shoulder to see the spark of another single candle flare into being. The dim light cast upon Gwen. She was holding a long, sharp sword.

****

Efar knew the second thief wasn't a flying creature, or he wouldn't have been riding. But he could still be a shapeshifter. Possibly a second werewolf. He'd have to plan this down to every fine detail.

He angled his wings to fly above his opposition. An attack from there wouldn't be expected. But, he had to time it carefully; otherwise one of the thieves would alert the other. His goal, therefore, was to take out the rider when attacking the dragon, all in one movement. And, of course, sometime during the fight, the dragon would have to let go of Captain.

As he flew, his wings sliced through the damp edge of a low cloud. He considered another problem: fire. Dragons ate phosphorous rock so they could spit fire. Would this one, a thief, have done that? Would he have had the money to buy some, or wanted to carry it with him? Would he have eaten it already, gambling that someone would attack him while he was shifted into his beast? Somehow, Efar felt the answers to all those questions were a resounding "No."

The dark shadow below changed course toward the west. Efar followed. So far, neither thief had thought to look up. Ahead, the moonlight glinted off a series of six lakes. This would be his best chance, before they had to rise for the mountains that marked the beginning of dragon territory.

Just as they crossed over the largest of the lakes, he dove toward the dragon's head, sweeping one wing against the rider and knocking him off. The thief fell with a scream. The dragon didn't drop Captain as hoped. It snaked its head toward Efar and hissed. Instinctively, Efar rolled away, but no fire came.

Again, he dove toward the dragon's head, clawing and pecking at its eyes. As long as it held Captain, there was little it could do other than snap at Efar if he flew too close. In an effort to escape, the dragon flew lower and lower until they were just above the tree line.

They passed the water and banks of the first lake, coming to the smaller second one. Efar backed off and the dragon took two mighty flaps. Then, it was over water again. Efar attacked. This time, the giant beast let go of the horse and turned belly up to counter the griffin's attack with claws, wings, and teeth of his own.

Efar, instead of joining combat with his enemy, tucked and rolled to the side, and then straightened out and rocketed after the plummeting Captain. In the brief span of the fall, he wondered at why he would risk so much for a woman he barely knew and who wasn't sure if she wanted his touch. There was one thing he didn't wonder about, though: Fiera would never forgive him if something happened to her horse.

Efar's plan was to follow Captain right into the lake and help the horse swim to land. His plan hadn't included the dragon, angry at the loss of its prize, diving after him. But, within seconds of Captain's feet touching water, the dragon barreled into Efar's back, driving him deep into the lake, all the way to the peat bottom.

In the dark water, Efar couldn't see what he was doing, where his enemy was, or if Captain made it to safety. The weight of the dragon forced all the air from Efar's chest as he lay trapped on the lake floor. His lungs ached from oxygen deprivation. His limbs felt heavy and his head grew fuzzy.

He had to do something or he'd die here, at the bottom of this lake. The dragon was big enough to keep its head above water. Squirming brought Efar no relief, nor did pushing with his legs. He tried swiping at the dragon's skin with his razor sharp eagle claws, but to no avail. The thick scales protected the beast. He faded in and out of consciousness.

He took one talon, reached up to the dragon's foot, and rammed it under the dragon's claw. The terrible crushing weight lifted off of him. With every last bit of strength funneled into his weak limbs, he pulled himself to the surface. His head broke above the water and he took in a great gulp of air, filling his lungs to their fullest capacity. He spread his wings like a raft, holding himself above the water. The dragon was grappling with Captain, trying to once again lift him.

Efar was in no shape for another speed flight, especially not one over the mountains. He had to stop this thief right here, right now. With a final burst of energy, he exploded into the night sky, directly in front of the giant beast. Stretching his neck, he hissed at the dragon, and then loosed with a primal scream that brooked no confusion. He tipped back and opened his talons with a *snick* and shoved them and his lion claws forward. He fanned his wings as large as he could, showing the heavy bone that could break a man's head. That dragon needed to know exactly what it'd be facing if it tried to take the horse.

The heavy monster hesitated. It was alone and far from anyone who would help. Bellowing back at Efar, it dropped the squirming and kicking Captain back in the water and arced neatly into the clouds above.

Efar landed in the mere beside the swimming horse and slowly changed back to human. He lay back in the water, drinking in air and staring at the quarter moon. His head buzzed and his limbs tingled from the unspent adrenaline.

How had he gotten into this mess? To the point of death? A woman. For him, it was always a woman. And this one was quite beautiful, or would be, once she got some meat on her bones. She was brave, strong, and smart, too. Quite a woman. Scratch that. Though she was old enough to be a woman, she was so naïve in the ways of the world, she could only be considered a child. Is that what he wanted for a mate? A child? Who knew how long it would take her to grow up?

No. He wasn't interested in a child, no matter how old she was. He was going to return Captain, because he said he would. Then he would just walk away and find his amusement elsewhere. Someday, he'd find the right woman to be his mate. Someone like Fiera, but more mature and knowledgeable.

With a grunt, he rolled over and began swimming toward shore. Captain was safe and they both needed food and rest. Then they'd head back to Chester.

****

Fiera jerked out of Laurence's grip. "I'm not going anywhere." She pivoted to face the witches.

Beside her, she was conscious of Laurence doing the same. He asked, "Gwen?"

The tall, thin woman lifted her face and studied Fiera. The candlelight deepened the hollows in her face, making her look almost cadaverous. After a moment, she nodded and returned to begin the ritual.

Laurence blew out his candle and whispered, "Stay quiet or else you'll disrupt the energy."

Fiera gave a single nod, though she knew he couldn't see it. She kept her gaze on the tableau in the center of the barn.

Facing north, Gwen raised her candle, speaking loudly. "I present this candle in the name of the Mighty Ones, past and present, male and female. May power and blessing descend upon this place and those gathered here."

She lit four more candles—Fiera thought they might be light blue or green, but it was difficult to tell in the dim light—none as big as the first, and placed one in each direction of the compass, outside the circle of stones. "I call upon you, Lords of the Watchtower, Lords of the Earth, Sky, Water, and Fire, to witness our rite and guard over our circle."

With that, the other witches came from the south and joined her around Marie. Gwen drew the tip of her sword mere inches above the stones in the circle, starting in the north. "I conjure the Circle of Power to be a boundary between the world of men and the realm of the Mighty Ones."

Goose bumps tingled across Fiera's skin as the power in the room built. She glanced at Laurence, now able to see him dimly from the light of five candles. His face was flushed and he stared at those within the circle with rapt attention, his eyes shining.

The witches in the center of the circle, men and women, spaced themselves equally as Gwen took the position to the north. They all closed their eyes, seeming to concentrate, some with hands toward Marie and some muttering softly to themselves.

Fiera's own magic hungered to enter into the circle, to be part of the wheel of power, and, if not for Laurence's hand on her arm, she would have joined them. No doubt to the ruination of the rite.

After a moment, Gwen raised her hands, her eyes still shut. "Oh, Mighty Ones, Lords of the Watchtower, heal Marie's body. Flow your energy into the wounds. Heal her torn flesh and bind her pain. Oh, Mighty Ones, heal your child well. This we desire. So shall it be." She fell into silence, once again joining the others in meditation.

Fiera felt her own magic expand and leap outward from its containment within her. Always a murky noise in the background of her mind, the voices of the animals that had been moved from the barn now became clear as if they were in congress right next to her. She felt her hair change color, of its own. She'd never felt it do that before.

Twice more, after a time of meditation, Gwen repeated her spell on Marie's behalf. With each incantation the power built within the barn until the air felt electric with it. Fiera could only imagine how strong it was within the circle.

By the time the witches filed out of the southern end of the circle, Fiera could clearly hear the thoughts of every animal in the city. Not only that, but she could single out a thought and follow it back to the individual. Her skin felt like it was alternately on fire and then doused with cooling rain.

"Wow," came Laurence's voice from beside her.

She turned and found him appraising her, his gaze roving up and down her, stopping at her hair. Self-consciously, she reached up and twitched a lock of it into her eyesight. Red. No surprise there. She supposed she'd have to change it back to brown when she'd decide to go among normal people again. It was all right for now, though. She raised her chin, suddenly very proud of being a witch.

But, the way Laurence kept looking over her made her glance at her clothes. They were still the same: torn and disheveled. Unnerved, she looked away from him to find Gwen approaching. The tall woman had the same look, although much more tired, as Laurence. She reached out and ran her hand down Fiera's hair. "Beautiful."

Gwen stepped back and also looked Fiera up and down. Several others came up behind her and stared. The tall witch said, "Let's go into the house and get something to eat. My servants will have cooked."

She reached out to slide her arm around Fiera's waist, but Fiera moved away. "I'm not leaving Marie."

The tall woman smiled. "You're a faithful friend. Mind the candles, but don't go near the circle. I'll be back in a moment. Then we can talk about what terrible thing happened in your past."

Chapter 6

Bartheleme arrived at his father's Chester home in the dark between midnight and dawn. They'd ridden straight through, disregarding those they passed when warned about thieves. Really, what was there for a dragon to fear? He almost relished a chance to let a little blood. Sadly, they'd reached the city gates unmolested.

Sitting in one of the heavy walnut chairs, he gazed around the lamp-lit great hall. His father had arranged it much the same way as the war room in the castle. More chairs, such as the one he sat in, lined the walls with thick tapestries hung between.

In fact, heavy everything was everywhere. The place felt small, too small for a dragon of his stature, but it was comfortable and he liked it. Instead of less, it felt like more. More comfort. More peace. More freedom from prying eyes.

His father's agent entered the room and bowed. "Your Highness."

Bartheleme waved his hand languidly, playing the role that would be his in a few centuries. "What is it?"

The fat man straightened, his calculating eyes meeting gaze for gaze. "No one has seen the two witches, My Prince."

"Not yet. But they're here."

"Yes, Sire. That is certain. We will find them." His air of conviction was absolute and Bartheleme trusted his father's agent would not fail the mission, knowing who the next king would be.

Bartheleme nodded as the fat man bowed again and left the room. The man was good at what he did. He had his own agents who, in turn, had those who worked for them. It was a net that would cast wide enough to catch one specific kind of witch. One who could expose the dragons' deepest kept secret.

His father's agent returned a few moments later, a robed woman beside him. Dark hair spilled from her head and down her back. The fat man bowed and said, "Sire, this woman brings news of the girls."

Bartheleme waved the agent away, stood, and approached the woman, who seemed to shrink within herself the closer he came. She was breathing hard and a fine sheen of perspiration covered her skin as if she'd hurried to share her news. He smiled as an encouragement. "You may feel comfortable here. We're all friends."

She curtseyed and he felt his smile deepen. There would be many such meetings with informants when he assumed the throne. The agents wouldn't be his father's, but his own. She said, "They've come to the meeting place. It's a barn behind the parish wife's home. One of the girls was badly injured. We prayed for her."

He glanced over her head at the fat man, who nodded, confirming he knew the location. Bartheleme returned his attention to the woman. He laid his hand on her shoulder. "Thank you. You need concern yourself with this no longer. Your service will be remembered."

"Bless you, Sire." The dark-haired woman blushed, bowed, and backed out of the room.

He turned to the agent and said, "We leave now. Get all the men you have."

****

Alone, Fiera walked to the edge of the circle and stared down at the body of Marie. The girl was still pale as death, her tiny chest not seeming to move with her breathing. The only obvious indication she was still alive were the occasional twitches of her fingers.

The candles burned in their assigned places, sending a heavy wax smell into the air, surrounding Fiera in the halo of their light. She lowered to the ground, as close as she could to the circle without touching it. She sent her own small prayer into the void of what she assumed must be the spirit world. "Mighty Ones, I'm new to you, as is Marie. And I know that's probably not her real name, but it's the only one I have for her. She's just a child, and so much bad has happened to her. Please, please, please heal her." She didn't quite know how to end it—her parents had never prayed with her—so, she just said, "Thank you."

Beside her, Gwen reappeared out of the gloom. She handed Fiera a plate of steaming vegetables and meat, and then settled beside her with another plate of her own.

Fiera picked up a piece of meat with her fingers and popped it into her mouth. It took no effort at all to chew and savory broth coated her tongue. She recognized the light musky flavor right away from her parents' table: lamb. The potatoes were braised: crunchy on the chopped edges and soft in the middle.

She motioned toward Marie and the circle. "Is it always like that? So powerful?"

Gwen shook her head, swallowing a bite. "Oh, no. We had our strongest healers inside. The need was great and, it seems, the Mighty Ones favor her."

The tall woman looked over at Fiera. "They favor you, as well."

Confusion filled Fiera. A spark of fear, too. What had she gotten into? Who were these Mighty Ones? Would they hurt her? "I...I don't understand."

Gwen sighed. "I'm sorry. This is all new to you, isn't it?"

At Fiera's quick smile, the parish wife continued. "Food and drink are not the only nourishments our bodies need. We also need companionship, happiness, and love. Without any of these our bodies begin to suffer. You lacked food. Your body shows obvious signs of starvation. But, that wasn't all you lacked. As witches, we also need to be surrounded by magic. When we aren't, it leaves a physical manifestation on us."

She paused to see if Fiera was following. At her nod, Gwen continued. "At my door, tonight, you showed clear indications of being near death, yourself. Your skin was thin and sallow. Your eyes were clouded and deep-set. Your cheekbones were pronounced. But, it's not so now. Your color is better and your skin looks fuller. Only one thing happened between the time you entered my home and now: magic. So, I ask you, what terrible thing happened in your past?"

Fiera blushed. It was true that during the fullness of power from the circle, her hair had returned to its natural fawn red. She looked at her arms. The skin looked more rosy than yellow. She even thought that her wrist bones didn't stick out quite as much, either. But had it really been enough of a change to warrant Laurence's reaction? And Gwen's?

She swallowed hard at the meat that had become

94

tasteless in her mouth. Her heart hammered against her ribs. "One day, when I was a child, a wagon rolled past our door, a large crowd following. In the wagon was tied a woman who looked just like me: red hair and green eyes. The crowd jeered and threw stones and waste at her. She was covered in manure, bruises, and cuts. She saw me and stared. That's when a large rock smashed against her head, killing her while she held my gaze. My family decided, that day, that it would be safer for me to never leave the house again. They told everyone I had died. They even had a funeral."

Gwen nodded slowly, her eyes filled with compassion. "You thought you saw your future in that poor woman. So, you've lived without magic all these years. Locked away because of it. That explains everything. You poor, poor girl." She pulled Fiera into an embrace and held her for a long moment.

Eventually, she pulled away, wiping her eyes, her voice thick with emotion. "Tell me how you ended up here, with Marie."

Fiera told the tale of her parents' deaths and how she'd run from her home, met Captain, rescued Marie, and befriended Efar. She didn't tell about Efar's griffin; that was his business if he wanted anyone to know. Then, she told of the werewolf attack.

Gwen asked, "This young man, Efar, has gone in search of your horse?"

Fiera nodded. "Efar will find him. He knows how much I care for Captain, even though the horse can be difficult at times. He saved my life."

Gwen paused, then said, "Witches usually have familiars who help them. They're sometimes demons, but often animals. It sounds like your horse is yours. And your young man seems to be more than just a traveling companion."

Fiera's face heated, remembering Efar's kiss and

his naked body. It was too embarrassing to face her new friend. She glanced away, but not quickly enough.

Gwen chuckled. "So, it's true then."

The whole thing with Efar confused Fiera. How was it that Efar's slightest glance warmed her from the inside out? That she still felt the trace of his finger on her cheek and she'd wanted to lean into him, even though she'd pulled away? That his kiss still burned her lips? How could she explain any of this, especially when Laurence's attention had done nothing for her? She shook her head and opened her mouth to speak, but was cut off by Laurence rushing into the barn, several acolytes behind him.

His words came out in a rush. "Gwen, there's a large contingency headed this way."

****

Efar crawled out of the mere and fell onto his back, staring at the sky. The stars were disappearing; dawn wouldn't be far away. Rolling over onto his side, he watched the shadow that was Captain. He had no troubles seeing the animal, his eyesight enhanced by the creature within him. Here, between the green growing trees, where the sun could warm the soil, grass grew lush and long. The horse ripped it by huge mouthfuls, often tearing the roots out of the ground as well. His long ears swayed flat out on either side of his head in a very undignified manner, and Efar suspected the horse had water in them.

Without looking at his human counterpart, Captain began walking east, jerking up the grass as he went, so that his front hooves almost clipped his jaw with every bite.

"Hey! Where are you going?" Efar jumped to his feet and ran after him. "Stop! At least let me get on.

Then we can collect clothes and some kind of bridle along the way."

When Captain didn't stop, Efar reached for the horse's withers, preparing to vault aboard.

In a snap, Captain whipped his head around, ears flat back against his skull, grass tumbling from his wide-open mouth, and thick, crushing teeth reaching for Efar's bare chest.

"Hey!" Efar jumped back, covering his chest with his hand, mostly to reassure he'd escaped unscathed. It'd been a close call; he'd actually felt the horse's whiskers brush across his skin. "I saved you! Without me, you'd be warming in a dragon's stomach by now."

Like a switch had been turned off, Captain returned to his grass-ripping walk.

Efar kept pace. "I can't walk the whole way. The forest will tear up my bare feet. I can fly, but if anyone sees you alone, you'll be captured again. Is that what you want? Do you even understand me or am I speaking aloud to myself?"

He stopped and stared, frowning, at the determination of the horse. After a moment, he called out, "Fiera's not where you left her. I had to move her and Marie."

Captain stopped dead at that, still facing the direction he'd been going, chewing on his most recent grass clump, a big ball of roots and dirt hanging out of his mouth.

"Oh, so you *can* understand me, you devil." Efar nodded and sauntered up to the horse's face, wagging his finger. "You don't know where I've taken them. You need me, don't you?"

The horse laid his ears back and swished his tail, but didn't offer to bite or kick.

"Okay. Since we're both trying to get to Fiera

and Marie, we'll have some rules. First, you're going to play nice."

Captain's tail swished harder and he stopped chewing. The mud lump fell to the ground, partially ground grass still attached.

"Second, you're going to let me ride. Is that clear? And, you're going to have to listen to what I say, or we won't get there at all." Efar paused to be sure his words sank in. Then, he boldly gripped Captain's withers and lifted himself onto the horse's back.

Immediately, he felt the horse's hip shift as he kicked right to where Efar had been standing a few seconds before. His statement was clear: he didn't like any of the rules.

"You couldn't quite help yourself, could you? That'll be the last of it, or we might as well part ways now."

Slowly, Captain's ears lifted from their plastered position against his skull. He waited quietly beneath Efar.

"I see we understand each other. Let's go back to where that fellow fell off the dragon. It's not too far away. Some of his clothes should fit and, hopefully, he'll have the rope they led you with."

With a final tail swish, Captain turned south. They traveled for only twenty minutes before they found the body of the fallen thief, his head horribly twisted at an impossible angle.

He dismounted and wiped horse hair from places that none should ever be. Then he inspected the thief's body.

The clothes were, of course, too small for Efar.

He pinched the bridge of his nose. There were no more clothes where they'd last camped, not that Captain would tolerate going even further out of the way. He eyed the angry, eating horse, who was slowly putting distance between them. Whatever did Fiera see in that animal? His estimation of her patience grew.

He shook his head and returned his attention to the problem of his clothing. Running his hands along the thief's beltline, he found a short dagger. Fingering the blade proved it was dull, but it should be sharp enough to cut thread and cloth. He smiled and bent to his task.

****

Fear gripped Fiera at Laurence's words.

Gwen pointed to two robed men. "Help me move Marie to one of the bedrooms in the house. Laurence, hide Fiera in the loft. The rest of you bring in the animals and cover the floor."

Everyone jumped into motion at once. Laurence snatched Fiera's hand and pulled her toward the loft ladder hidden against the front wall. As they climbed Fiera looked over her shoulder. Gwen was muttering a soft prayer over Marie. When she finished, she walked the circle, blowing out the candles. For a brief moment, they were surrounded in darkness. Fiera stopped dead, her breath echoing off the barn wall in front of her. Then light grew in the great center of the barn as lamps were lit and hung on the supporting posts around the edges. When Gwen placed the last one, she looked up at Fiera. "It'll be all right."

Fiera hesitated and then nodded. She would trust Gwen in this. After all, her new friend had been doing this whole witch thing for a long time. She continued her climb. As she reached the top of the ladder, she looked down again.

One of the two hand-picked men lifted Marie while the other collected the still-smoldering candles. Gwen led them toward the house, even as the animals were herded into the wide-open barn. Most of the animals went directly to individual stalls. However, one horse decided to join a fellow in a stall not his own. While a couple of Gwen's followers sorted them out, others scattered the swept-up straw, once again covering the star in the middle of the floor.

Meanwhile, the rest of the people changed into regular clothes and hid their robes in places in the barn from which they removed musical instruments. They set up the impromptu band in the center of the barn, right over the straw-covered star, and began playing a dancing melody.

Laurence led Fiera across the loft to the corner furthest from the house. He raised a board from the loft floor, revealing a small box about twelve inches deep, two feet wide, and six feet long. "No one knows about this space except Gwen and I. You'll be safe here."

Frowning and hesitant, Fiera lowered herself into the hole that more closely resembled a coffin than a hiding place. As soon as she was settled, Laurence replaced the board, stamping hard on it where the nails held it in place. "One of us will be back for you soon."

With that, he left amidst a shower of straw dust that made Fiera want to sneeze. She pinched her nose and breathed through her mouth, silently praying there were no spiders occupying the close quarters with her.

Light filtered through narrow cracks below her. Peering through, however, all she could make out was a horse shifting in its stall. She'd have to settle for just listening to the action. Slowly, Fiera shifted so her ear was pressed against one of the cracks.

Within moments, the music stopped to be replaced with the noise of many men. One voice carried in the barn better than the others. "You are the parish wife?"

"I am." It was Gwen's voice that answered, matching the man's strength with her own. "And who

100

might you be?"

"Who I am makes no difference. It's the two girls you have as guests here that matter. Where are they?"

"One is injured, near death. She sleeps in my house guestroom. The other has left."

"Left? Where did she go?"

"I don't know. It's none of my concern."

"I feel you're hiding something. Perhaps even this girl. Look around."

With a start, Fiera realized he'd said this last to his men. Immediately, she heard scuffs below her as well as footsteps on the loft ladder.

The man continued, "Tell your musicians to move."

Gwen's voice came sharply, "Do as he requests."

An awful feeling built in the pit of Fiera's stomach. If the star was found, Gwen and her followers would be shown as witches and would be arrested. Perhaps she could help. The wood she hid within was buried deep into the dirt the star was also buried into. She closed her eyes and pushed her magic through the loft floor, down the wooden posts, and along the ground toward the star, imagining a flat expanse of dirt instead of the stones. She felt the drawing of her power, but, without seeing the result, had no idea if it worked or had distorted somehow.

She sent a message to the horse below. *Hello horse. Can you tell me what is happening in the center of your barn?*

Lots of people. They sweep the barn floor. I wish they'd leave so I could sleep.

What do they find beneath the straw?

Nothing. Just dirt.

Who are the people there?

My owner and the one called Laurence. A few of

101

their friends. I don't know the others, but one smells really bad.

Is there a fat man?

Yes, but he doesn't smell. It's the tall, thin one.

A smelly man? Did her new four-legged friend mean a shapeshifter? No doubt he was, since he was in the company of what Efar had been sure was an agent for dragons. Was the tall thin man a dragon? *Will you tell me if something happens? If they take away your owner?*

Too noisy to sleep, anyway. The conversation reminded Fiera of Captain, and then quite suddenly of Efar. Her heart squeezed tight at the memory of his kiss. She missed him...them...them. She missed them.

Footsteps crossed the loft above Fiera and she slowed her breath.

✳✳✳✳

Efar undressed the fallen thief's body. The boots wouldn't fit, no matter what he might try. Neither would the tunic, but he'd learned how to make do with small clothes before. The pants, however, were quite usable. As peasant's clothes, they were roomy in the hip so as to allow a great range of motion while working. It was the waist that was a problem. That, and the length. But, there was nothing to be done about that.

Removing the rope that belted the pants, he cut the seams a couple inches down from the waistline. He pulled the pants on, tied them, and flexed his knees. He nodded with satisfaction. They were snug, but so were those of the fashion of high-court leggings.

He scooped up the tunic and turned toward his retreating ride. "Captain, I see you sneaking away. I'm ready. Let's go find our girls."

At the word "our," the horse's ears momentarily

flattened against his skull, then lunged upright again. He stopped walking.

As Efar swung onto the animal's wide back, Captain swished his tail and stepped into him, causing him to land ungracefully, scrambling to stay aboard. Once righted, Efar wryly said, "Nice try. Chester is northeast of us now, and a lot closer than our camp was. We should be there by nightfall. Assuming you don't dawdle."

Captain stepped off smartly, his tail swinging with each stride.

Efar cut the arms off the tunic and opened the seams down the sides. He pulled it over his head and then began working on the sleeves. The first one, he divided in half lengthwise. Tying the ends together, he created a sash and wrapped it around his waist.

The other sleeve, he cut into strips and braided them together into a cloth rope. This, he fashioned into a type of war bridle with one rein. Leaning forward, he dropped it over Captain's head. After tucking the knife into his new belt, he said to his mount, "If you're up to it, let's increase the speed."

The horse's ears flicked back briefly and then pointed forward with a purpose. Immediately, Captain picked up a trot, bouncing harshly across the ground.

Efar, caught unprepared for the extreme roughness of the gait, grappled to stay on the animal's back. He fisted huge chunks of mane and squeezed his legs tight. "Hey! Either take a faster gait, like a gallop, or back it down to a walk. I can't ride this."

Captain picked up his pace, but didn't break into another gait. The roughness increased.

"Fine. If you want me to treat you like any other horse, I will." Efar pushed his heels against the horse's ribs and made kissing noises with his mouth.

Captain's stride stretched out and he fell into a

ground-eating lope toward Chester.

****

Bartheleme stared at the dirt floor of the barn. He was sure, from what the witch acolyte had said, that he would find a large star and circle imbedded in the ground. From the sharp intake of breath of the tall parish wife beside him, he could assume she expected to see it as well.

He pivoted on his heel to look at her. It wasn't often a woman was tall enough he could look her directly in the eye. Her face was pale and she stared at the bare dirt. Slowly, she turned her gaze onto him.

"Where's the second witch?" he asked.

The woman shook her head. "I told you, she's not here." She held his gaze with confidence.

He nodded. Movement in the loft caught his attention. Above the nosy horses, one of the agent's men appeared at the edge and shook his head. Two more men came in from the back pasture, the brilliant pink of sunrise streaking westward across the sky behind them. They also shook their heads. Nothing.

Turning back to the parish wife, he said, "Show me the other." Obediently, she led the way. As they passed the fat agent, Bartheleme said to him, "Keep them searching. Broaden the area."

The fat man bowed his understanding and Bartheleme continued behind the tall woman. She led him into the house and upstairs to a bedroom dimly lit.

He recognized the witch's circle of candles, though it had been made to look random, and the blue candle of healing near the prone child's head. The girl was small with tousled brown curls and a white bandage across the breadth of her body. A sheen of sweat glistened on her skin and her breathing was shallow and

104

rough, at times catching in silence. She was very near death.

He glanced at the parish wife, then back at the girl, saying, "You know where the other girl is hiding. It would be better for you if you told me."

The woman raised her chin fractionally. "I don't know."

Bartheleme closed his eyes and faced her. Why was she making this so difficult? Opening his eyes again, he moved to within inches of her face. She held her ground. Impressed, he nonetheless said, "You think you're safe because you keep what you are as a secret. I suggest you are *not* safe; you have no idea who I am." He paused to let that sink in, then again asked, "Where is the second girl?"

Her face paled, but she held her tongue, meeting his gaze with large, wary eyes in the tight space between them. In that moment of silence, the girl's faint breaths filling the background, he understood the witch standing in front of him would never tell him what he needed so desperately to know.

He pointed at the unconscious child. "Make sure she lives, Witch." With that, he stepped around her and left the room. Downstairs, instead of returning to the barn, he went out the front of the house in the dawning light. He ground his teeth and paced up and down the street. His men would find nothing, no matter how long or thoroughly they searched. They were wasting their time. Yet, he felt sure the girl he wanted was hidden on the premises, somewhere.

The fat agent joined him. "My sincerest apologies, Sire. We've been unable to find her."

Bartheleme stopped and stared thoughtfully at the house. "Did your informant sneak back into the group safely?"

"Yes, My Lord. She'll keep us apprised if the
105

girl reappears."

Nodding, Bartheleme said, "Take your men home. I wish to walk alone."

As the agent's men gathered out front in preparation of their march back, Bartheleme turned toward the center of town. He often walked when he needed time to think and plot his next step. This time, he also needed time to lose the anger that had slowly been building within him since he'd started this undertaking.

****

The footsteps above Fiera had stayed a long time, walking back and forth, kicking, tromping, and sweeping straw dust down on her. She still had to keep her nose pinched the whole time, breathing through her mouth, just to keep from sneezing. Eventually, the feet left and all was quiet.

Horse, what's happening now?

Everyone has gone. My owner went off with the smelly man.

If she doesn't return, I'll feed you, don't worry.

You're a nice person. You must have horses of your own.

She did. Or, rather, she had a horse friend. And a shapeshifter friend. All her life, she'd believed shifters were myths or hallucinations. Now, in the space of a day, she'd come into contact with three. What did they want?

Blushing furiously, she amended her question. She was pretty sure what Efar wanted, and the werewolf had wanted Captain, but what about this last one, this tall thin man? What did he want?

It had all started when she'd stolen Marie. Her heart hammered against her ribs. Had they taken her as well? She'd tear Chester apa—

106

The board above her suddenly lifted off, sending more straw dust into her hiding place. She'd lapsed in her nose pinch and she sneezed loud enough it echoed off the barn walls.

"Bless you."

Fiera twisted around to her back to be greeted by Laurence silhouetted in the dim morning light. He said, "They're gone."

"Marie?" She took his outstretched hand, letting him help her to her feet and out of the box.

"She's in the house."

Dropping his hand, she hurried to the ladder. Halfway down, she slipped in her haste and skinned her shin scrambling for the nearest rung. By the time she reached the bottom, shaking had settled under her skin as much from the fright of the near fall as from her anxiety over her young friend.

She ran into the house and up the steps. Three doors faced her. Taking a gamble, she opened the first to her right. There, looking smaller than normal under a giant bed quilt was the pale form of Marie.

Fiera breathed a sigh of relief at finding her friend. A split second before she stepped into the room, a hand gripped her arm. Whirling around, she met Gwen's stern gaze.

"Don't go in there until I show you how. You'll break the circle and lose the energy," the tall woman said. "First though, tell me the identity of those men."

Fiera shook her head. "I don't know any names and I've only seen the fat man before. He followed me and Marie for a while yesterday morning. We didn't see him anymore after that."

Gwen pressed her lips together and stared at the wall with a far-off look in her eyes.

Fiera hesitated, then said, "Efar thinks the one we saw may be an agent for a dragon lord."

The parish wife's gaze snapped to her. "Dragons. Loathsome beasts. Why would they want you?"

"It's Marie they want. The agent was already at the inn where I found her."

Smiling sadly, Gwen rubbed Fiera's arm. "You're the one they kept asking about."

Despite her best efforts, Fiera felt her courage leach away. "M...me? Why would they want me?"

The tall woman opened her mouth as if to say something and hesitated. Then her frown smoothed and she said, "We'll figure that out later. Right now, you need rest. Come, you can sleep beside your friend. I'll rebuild the circle after you're in."

****

Efar and Captain traveled through the day. The sky was overcast, blocking the heat of the sun. Humidity was slowly building, but it wasn't uncomfortable. They changed pace often, Efar occasionally dismounting to walk beside his four-legged companion, but they never stopped. They mostly stayed at an evenly paced trot, Efar bouncing like a raisin in a basket. The trot was a ground-eating pace that Captain was able to sustain much longer than a gallop. There seemed to be a burning need within the horse to reach Fiera. Efar felt it, too.

At the beginning of dusk, they reached the south bridge that crossed the river Dee and led into Chester. The line to enter the city gate stretched all the way across the bridge. Thankful for an excuse to stop, Efar dismounted. He felt completely raw from exhaustion and, glancing at Captain's hanging head, knew the horse felt the same. He patted the animal on the shoulder. For the first time, Captain didn't pin back his ears. Efar smiled. It may be the horse didn't react because of weariness, but it was promising for their friendship.

No, thought Efar. He'd already forgotten his earlier vow to return the horse to its owner, then continue on his way, alone. There would be no friendship, no dalliance, no invitations. He was disappointed with his failure to remember something so important to his future. He meant to stick to it, now.

By the time they reached the gate and its guards, dusk was long gone and they were once again locked in the dark of night. The dancing lamplights from the city held the blackest of the shadows at bay, but most crept in at odd angles and held Chester in their grip.

Before Efar could say anything to the guards, one who had been looking him up and down asked, "You're not a Dane. But, where are your shoes, Sir?"

Efar glanced at the thick tall man, and answered the question with a question. "What does it matter?"

"Well, a man of your obvious standing, dressed in courtly fashion, appears without shoes and it makes me wonder what the story is."

The second guard, built much like the first, chimed in. "Or, if he's really just a thief who's stolen a nobleman's finery and horse."

The people in line behind Efar backed away. He said, "If I were a thief, I wouldn't have come to this gate, the busiest in the city. I would have entered through one of the various other methods thieves use."

The guards grudgingly looked at each other. The first said to the second, "He's got a point, but it still doesn't explain the shoes."

The second answered, "They probably didn't fit when he stole them." They both turned expectantly to Efar.

He dropped his gaze to his feet and chuckled at himself. Stopped because of a pair of shoes. He shook his head at his bad luck. It had all been bad since he'd met those kids and the horse beside him. Didn't matter,

109

though. He had to get inside the city and return the horse. If he let himself be taken, Captain would be confiscated. Fiera would never know he was safe and Efar's promise to her would be broken.

He looked up at the two guards and smiled as sheepishly as he could. Leaning close, he winked and spoke in a low voice, as if he were trying to keep anyone else from hearing. Not that he really cared if anyone overheard his tale. "The truth is, fellows, that I fancy a game of chance now and then. Traveling gets tedious, especially when alone. I stopped at a little burg called Midden and sported in a game with a few of the occupants at the inn. Sadly, I lost every bit of coin I owned. I had to trade my boots for this horse. They were fine boots, too. From Spain. Made from the finest kidskin, tanned under a dry Tuscan sun. They had golden buckles—"

"Go on." The second guard irritably waved him into the city, shaking his head, disgust written on his face.

The first one added, "If you fancy a game, again, I like to relax at the Troubadours' inn outside the east gate."

Efar nodded, trying to look excited at the prospect of meeting up with the guard, and led Captain through the stone gate into Chester proper. Now, how to find Fiera? If he'd asked at the gate, it would have given him away.

A man pulling a cart approached with a woman by his side. Two small children rode in the cart atop a full load of drought-dwarfed potatoes. They were headed toward the gate, no doubt to trade with the boat merchants.

Efar gave his friendliest smile. They slowed. Two small pairs of eyes gazed at him from the cart. The woman blushed, as most did when they met him, and the

110

man regarded him with suspicion, also as most men with women did. Both glanced quickly at his hair. Efar asked, "Could you tell me where injured people are taken?"

The man's voice was hard. "To one of the churches, I expect." He picked up his pace again.

"Please. It's just...my wife brought our child here and I don't know where they were taken. Can you help me?" Efar spoke to them in general, but his gaze rested on the wife.

She laid her hand on her husband's arm and he stopped with a questioning look at her. To Efar, she said, "Mostly they're taken to the big monastery near the end of this road."

He waved his thanks, sprung up on Captain, and hurried down the road. Looking back, as the cart passed under a lamp, he saw it was at full speed again and the two children were watching him intently. Then they were gone from sight, swallowed by the dark.

Even after nightfall, Chester streets were busy. Because of the boat merchants docking at all hours, the city never really slept. Keeping Captain at a trot proved to be impossible and twice they had to stop all together because the traffic was so congested. After the main crossroads between all the gates, however, the way cleared and Efar was able to pick up the pace until he reached the side entrance onto the monastery's property. From then, it was just a few moments until he reached the front entrance where he tied Captain to a hitching post.

The building was impressive in size; he'd seen many castles smaller. The central door was framed in a tall tower. Two double story arms extended straight out to the sides, presumably to house monks and visiting clergy. The lowest level, below ground would be where the infirm were held and that's where he rushed when he entered.

111

He didn't understand the frantic feeling he had to see Fiera and Marie again. It was new, something he'd never experienced before. It surprised him, after all the years of his life, that he should be overwhelmed by a feeling for two girls he swore he was leaving. It had to be because of Marie's condition when he'd last seen her. But that reasoning sounded hollow, even to him.

Striding rapidly down the central aisle, he glanced left and right, whipping aside partitions, searching pale, sickly faces, but to no avail. He reached the end of the hospital and had seen neither Marie nor Fiera.

The fever pitch of urgency rose into fear.

A monk approached from the far end and Efar, swallowing his feelings hard, walked to meet him. "There was an injured girl brought in last night. She was badly mauled by a wild beast. A woman was with her."

The monk nodded. "Yes. There were here, but they left. We don't know what became of them. But, I doubt that girl lived. She was near death when she arrived." He continued on his path.

Efar stood in the aisle, heartsick. Marie dead? It couldn't be.

He'd experienced people passing before, even loved ones, but this hit him hard. And he'd only known her a day. The frantic urgency within him suddenly appeared again as a near panic. Fiera! She'd be devastated. He had to find her.

He hurried back to the main floor and out the front door of the building. Standing on the stoop, he gazed at the lamps of the city. So many. And beneath them, a mass of people. He had no idea where she could be.

As he untied Captain, he said, "Call Fiera in your mind. Perhaps she'll hear you."

A few seconds later, the horse started walking

down the monastery drive toward the street where he turned east, only to shortly turn south again on the next road. Efar walked beside him, holding the reins, trying to make it appear as if he were leading the horse, not the other way around. He caught a few curious stares, but most people didn't seem to notice.

A young woman ran toward them, flashing in and out of pools of lamp light. She had the same fawn-red hair as Fiera and was wearing the same clothes he'd last seen her wearing, but this couldn't be her.

The gauntness of her frame was gone. While still thin, it was fuller, rounder. Her face was softer. She looked older than before, reaching her full nineteen years of age. He had no idea how she could have changed so much overnight like that, but he heartily approved.

She ran right up to him and wrapped her arms around him in an embrace, leaning her head against his shoulder.

Efar's heart battered his ribs and his mouth dried.

****

Fiera hadn't planned on hugging Efar, but when she saw him, something took hold of her. All reason had failed and she'd ended up in his arms. It felt good there: solid, safe, and...exciting. All at once. She breathed in the natural wild musk of him. A warm fire built beneath her skin, spreading to her belly and other parts of her body.

With regret, she pulled away, unable to meet his gaze. She concentrated on Captain instead, leaning her small forehead against his giant one. *Hello, friend! I've missed you!*

Friend? Really? I'm not just your horse?

Of course, Silly. Do you think Efar would have

113

gone after you if you were just my horse?

Humph! The things he put me through!

We'll talk about it later. She reached up to stroke his neck, letting her magic flow over him. *I'm giving back your color before something interrupts us. It should be safe, now.*

Captain raised his head high and twisted to look down his long body. *My dapples! They're back!* He bobbed his nose in excitement.

Fiera finally turned her gaze back to Efar, expecting to see amusement in his ever-dancing blue eyes, but they were still and filled with sorrow. His mouth was downturned.

He took her hands in his. "I'm so, so sorry about Marie."

She frowned. Marie? Did he feel it was his fault she was injured? Her heart melted and she smiled softly. "It's all right. You couldn't have stopped it from happening. She's healing well and I'm told she'll wake soon."

His eyes widened and his shoulders relaxed. "She's alive?"

Surprised, Fiera nodded. Someone must have told him otherwise. "She is. Would you like to see her? Or do you prefer to stand out here all night?" She turned to lead the way, not waiting for an answer, knowing it already.

Efar let go of one hand as she turned, holding Captain's reins in it, but he held tightly onto her other hand, as if afraid she'd be stolen from him any instant.

They walked a few steps in silence. Tension built within her, the heat of his hand burning hers. His nearness captured her every heartbeat. She sought frantically for something to say. Finally, she stopped, pulling him to a stop as well, looking him up and down. "Now, I have a question for you: what are you wearing?"

Before Efar could answer, Captain's voice butted into her head. *Naked! He rode me naked! Such humiliation!*

Uncontrollable giggles bubbled out of Fiera at Captain. *Shush!*

Efar blushed, assuming the giggles were aimed at him. "I had to make do," he mumbled.

She laughed loudly, pulling them to a walk again. "You have to tell me what happened. I'm getting bits and pieces from Captain, but..." She shrugged.

Efar rolled his eyes. "That horse! He was so much trouble, I would have left him half a dozen times if I hadn't promised you I'd bring him back." As they walked to the parish house, he told her his story, interjected with comments from Captain in her mind.

When he finished, she was laughing so hard she couldn't walk and was nearly bent double with her free arm wrapped around her waist to help relieve the laugh cramps. Eventually she straightened. In between bouts of mirth, she said, "All Captain kept saying was, 'Stinky, wet, and naked!' He said it the whole time you were talking."

Wonder on his face, Efar watched her. "You're not the same girl I met at the crossroads. You've changed, more than just your appearance.

She wiped her eyes, still chuckling, and began walking again. After a moment she told her side of the story. He listened with rapt attention. Even Captain kept quiet. She finished by saying, "That's why I've changed. Gwen says I was starved for magic, but it's more than that. I'm finally free to be who...what I am. They accept me here. They even encourage me. I can learn spells and Marie can learn potions."

"So, we're going to be here a while."

She looked over at him, confused and frowning.

115

"We?"

He stopped under a street lamp and pulled on her hand, bringing her up against him. He ran his free hand through her hair. His eyes grew smoky grey, looking dangerous and exciting all at the same time. "Yes, we. You don't think I'm going to let anyone keep us apart now, do you?" He dropped Captain's reins and cupped his hand behind her neck. Leaning in to her, he tenderly touched his lips to hers. Then, as she responded with her own kiss, he pressed harder, letting go of her hand to circle her waist, pulling her tighter against him.

It was as if the spark that had been dancing around her stomach since the moment she'd seen him again had landed and burst into open flame. Her body fanned into a burning heat and, of its own, pressed against him. Her arms circled his neck and her fingers tangled in his hair. Their lips moved together in unison.

His breaths came thick and heavy, hers just as dense. His tongue flicked across her lips and she offered him entrance, her tongue darting out to meet his, wrapping around and around, twisting and turning, like some kind of wild animal.

It felt as if she'd fallen through the crust of the earth and found something akin to Heaven. It felt wonderful, and yet, it frightened her. She'd never been this close with anyone. Was it real? Would it last? Fiera dropped her hand to Efar's chest and gently pushed away. As their lips parted, it felt as if he dragged her soul with him. His breath was ragged, matching hers, and his eyes had dropped to a near black. She said softly, "I'm not used to this."

He nodded slowly, playing with a tendril of her hair, concentrating on it. Then he focused his gaze on her. "I'm not going to hurt you."

She smiled at him. "I know. I've led such a sheltered life that I've not had much to do with romance.

116

But, I know what I feel right now, for you, isn't something that happens often."

"Shapeshifters live for a long time. I've been alive for almost two hundred years now and I can say that I've never felt this way before, either." He pulled her close and kissed her again.

She pressed hard against him, opening her mouth hungrily and darting her tongue forward to meet his. With a muffled moan, he crushed her to him.

****

Efar drank in Fiera's scent. It surrounded him like a fog. He hadn't lied when he said he'd never felt as he did now. It had taken him almost two hundred years to find the woman who loved him and also captured his beast's attention.

He held her against his body as tightly as he could, yet it wasn't enough. His body's need was hard upon him, but it was his soul that cried for more. He felt ravenous for her love, as if he could devour her. And from her response, she felt the same for him.

This woman was the one he would die for. Anything she needed would be his task to find. Forever. He would vanquish any foe, even 1000 dragons, to keep her safe. Speaking of which, now wasn't the time for romancing.

Reluctantly, he pulled away. "Let's discuss this fellow who's been asking about you. What did he look like?" He took her hand and, together, they walked down the road again. Captain followed, dragging his reins.

"I don't know what he looks like. Just tall and thin. I was hidden by the time he came into the barn. But Gwen could tell you."

"You said the agent was with him?"

"I assume he was the fat man." They reached the next road and Fiera turned right, pulling Efar with her. Glancing up at the houses, her step faltered.

Efar gripped Fiera's arm, following her line of sight. With his enhanced vision, he saw someone tall and thin approaching on the darkened road. A woman. She looked to stand at least a head taller than any of his brothers. She had a slow, stately walk, sure of herself. He whispered to Fiera, "Who is it?"

"I don't know. I can't see very well." The arm beneath his hand shivered.

Before he could answer, the woman called out to them in a strong voice. "Fiera, Marie's awake!"

"That's Gwen." Relief coursed through Fiera's voice. She started to pick up her pace again, but Efar held her back. The only people he knew that tall were dragons.

He kept his voice low, in her ear. "Ask Captain what she smells like."

"What?" Fiera stared hard at him. "That's Gwen. She's my friend. I have to get to Marie."

"Just ask him." He moved to be in between the two women, gently pushing Fiera behind him. If this woman was a dragon, he had to be ready. He embraced the griffin within him, ready to jump into the beast at a split-second's notice. His skin tingled in anticipation.

She was silent a moment, then answered with exasperation in her voice, "He says she smells pretty."

Pretty. Efar nodded to himself and relaxed. No dragon smelled pretty.

"But," Fiera continued, an edge of panic creeping into her voice, "He says there's someone else nearby who *does* stink. And he says it's not you."

Efar pushed her behind him again, circling so that her friend, Gwen, was also behind him. He peered into the darkness. Even with his vision, he saw no one.

That didn't mean anything; there were so many hiding places around the clustered houses.

Captain bolted back the direction from which they'd come, his hooves throwing great clods of dirt behind him.

Efar turned to face the darkness and the unseen menace from which the horse fled. They'd been walking right to it. No doubt it had followed Gwen. Was she a collaborator? Surely she would smell, even a bit, if she were. He bellowed into the night, "Show yourself, Dragon! Or are you too cowardly?"

****

Bartheleme smiled to himself. The girl, whom he'd learned was named Fiera, was a rare gem, drawing friends to her like a magnet. Friends that lied for her and would defend her. Even now, the tall witch he'd met earlier was muttering a protection spell beside the man he knew as Efar.

He stepped out of the shadows and approached, watching the face of the girl. Unlike the man she loved, whose face was filled with suspicion, or the tall witch who was obviously afraid, the girl was curious and more than a little defiant. Though he spoke to Efar, he kept his gaze locked on Fiera. "I'm no coward...griffin. Yes, I know who you are. I know all seven of your brothers and your mother's uncle, who is the king of all your kind. If you knew who I am, you wouldn't dare to speak that word to me."

He stopped ten feet away from the trio. Shifting his gaze to Efar, he watched with satisfaction as the possibilities clicked through the man's mind and settled on one with widened eyes.

The griffin spoke slowly, couching his words. "My apologies, My Lord, but we had no way of knowing what manner of man lay hidden here."

Bartheleme ground his teeth. It was true the royalty of shifter families rarely bowed to each other. Still, it would have been proper if the griffin had shown a little deference. And the apology was barely that, if at all. It contained a double insult, first in insinuating he was a mere man, not shifter royalty. Second, in suggesting he *was* a coward for hiding.

He held back his rebuke, however. This was not the time for a fight. He'd only stumbled upon the little group because he'd been standing outside the parish house, considering options, when the tall witch had rushed out. It had been a simple matter to follow her. But he had no men with him. Though he could easily handle the griffin, the girl would likely run off in the commotion. No, he would not provoke an all-out fight.

Fiera had moved out from behind Efar, staring at him with insolence.

There was only one way to find out if someone was a mind speaker.

While your witch friend has been out here, my men have taken the little girl. I'll kill her if you don't come with me quietly. Don't say a word.

Fiera's eyes flew wide open.

****

Fiera stared at the tall thin man before her, not answering, not moving. He had Marie! She couldn't let anything happen to her young friend. Even if it cost her own life. Yet, she couldn't bring herself to step away from Efar's side.

I have your little friend, his voice came in her head again. He said nothing out loud, but he kept his gaze locked with hers. He'd spoken in her mind. Only animals could do that. Or was it something that had

120

come with the surge of magic?

The man didn't look like a dragon; he was too skinny. In fact, he more closely resembled Gwen. Now she understood Efar's curious behavior regarding the witch.

She pushed aside the panic building within her. Was it possible he didn't know she could hear him? A fishing expedition?

She called out to him. "What do you want?"

I know you can hear me. I saw your reaction when you heard me. If you don't leave with me right now, I'll make sure they all die. Remember, one word and I'll kill them all.

Fiera's pulse rang in her ears. Her breaths came rapid and shallow. The panic inside her began building again and she knew she had to act before it took over. Biting her lip, she stepped forward, eyes on the ground. Her legs felt like jelly.

Efar reached for her arm, but she jerked away. How could she walk away from him without a word, after that kiss? Did she have a choice? There was no doubt in her mind the dragon man could do what he said. She had to do this.

She took another step. And another.

"Fiera!" Efar reached for her again, confusion plain in his voice.

Again, she pulled away from him and continued, until she stood before the dragon man. He gripped her arm and led her down the street, away from her friends, away from the man she loved.

Would this be the last time she saw them? Efar? Unbidden, the panic surged into anger. To her friends, it would have looked like she'd abandoned them. Betrayed them.

The dragon man's grip tightened on her arm as the fat agent disengaged from the shadows down the street and met them. He turned to walk with them.

The man who held Fiera said, "You know what to do. He's a griffin, so use your bows."

The fat man nodded and hurried back toward Efar and Gwen. More men appeared, some pulling bows, arrows, and swords as they followed the agent.

Fiera jerked on her arm, but it was held like a vise. "You're going to kill them anyway!"

He looked down at her for the first time since he'd taken her and, though it was dark, she read something...sad...in his eyes. "Yes. I'm sorry, but it's necessary." He picked up the pace.

At a half-run to match his long strides, she asked, "Necessary? Why? For what?"

He pressed his mouth into a thin line and didn't answer.

There had to be something she could do! How could she warn Efar? Would the man beside her hear if she spoke to Captain? There was only one way to find out. While watching the dragon man, she spoke to the horse. *Can you hear me?*

Captain answered immediately. *Fiera, where are you? I was so scared! How'd you get away from the dragon?*

The dragon man gave no hint he'd heard a single bit of the conversation.

Captain, listen. This is important. The dragon man has taken me as his prisoner. He already has Marie. He's sent soldiers to kill Efar and Gwen. Find a way to help them. Then you have to convince them to follow you to where I'm going to be held.

The horse didn't respond.

Captain, do you understand?

There was a long moment of silence before the horse answered. *I have to fight? Are they shifters?*

You're a war horse. Act like one.

122

Fine! But no one better eat me.

Fiera closed her eyes, rushing along at the dragon man's side. Even in a crisis the horse was difficult. Well, it was the best she could do for her friends until she could get herself and Marie free.

She sensed a change in the air around her and she popped open her eyes again. The man beside her was growing at a fantastic rate. Not as fast as she'd seen Efar, but still quick. His clothes were splitting, not just at the seams, but right across the cloth. His head and neck became long like a horse, only finer. Lizard-like skin covered wings that sprouted from his shoulder blades, pushing the shreds of his tunic off, while sharp bumps rose from his backbone. His pants tore apart from the width of his legs and the tail protruding from the top of his hips.

Long scythe-like claws pushed out from the hand that gripped her arm. The hand grew larger and larger, until it completely engulfed her whole arm. The dragon was huge! She'd never seen any living thing so large. It was bigger than Gwen's barn, by far. And, she almost thought its skin was blue. But that could have been her imagination.

It wrapped its clawed hand around her waist and lifted into the night sky.

Chapter 7

Efar had watched slack-jawed as Fiera, the woman he loved and who somehow made sense as a mate to his griffin, had walked away beside Dragon Prince Bartheleme, only son of King Cynan The Mighty. With his eagle vision, he had followed their progress until they stepped beneath a lamplight and spoke with the fat agent who'd been plaguing Fiera since Midden. Then, as the two continued on, the agent strode toward where Efar waited with Gwen. Now, men joined from the shadows, pulling long swords and more than a few dangerous bows.

Efar turned to Gwen. "Get Marie and hide where no one will find you. Then, in a day or two, when they stop looking for you, head southeast out of town into the griffin territory. Tell them Efar sent you."

Panic filled her eyes as she, too, saw the approaching mob, but she remained rooted to the spot. "What about you?"

He turned from her, back to watch the oncoming group of armed men as it continued to swell. "I'll hold them off so you have enough time. Then, I mean to find

124

out what's going on with Fiera. Now, Run!" Without waiting to see if she obeyed, he exploded into the griffin.

He'd never shifted that fast and the pain lanced through the marrow of his bones, raced through his body like a raging fire, and scored his mind. He would have fallen if not for the instincts of the beast. All around him, tiny tatters of his makeshift clothing flittered to the ground like snowflakes. Beside him, he heard the tall woman gasp. Then she ran.

Gathering his senses, Efar charged the oncoming horde. He stayed on the ground so the arrows wouldn't do as much damage and he could use the men in front as cover as he rushed them, putting every ounce of energy into his legs. At the last second, he raised mere inches off the ground, tucking his head and legs beneath his wings, and bowled right into the center mass, knocking men left and right. Snapping his wings open, he clubbed any unlucky soul nearby who rose, while he snaked his neck around to grip the fat agent's shoulder with his beak, crushing it with a satisfying crunch. The man dropped to the ground beside his sword, screaming.

The sound of charging hooves reached his ears above the cries of the injured men. Then, a pair of dark grey hooves crashed down on the head of an archer from the edge of the mass.

Captain!

Faced with two adversaries, most of the attacking men hesitated for a brief second, trying to decide which was the most formidable. That was all Efar needed. He sucked in a great draft of air and bellowed a war cry as loud as he could. The sound echoed off the nearby buildings, amplifying the ferocity. Many men covered their ears. Most ran. The few that remained dropped their weapons and hesitantly reached to help the injured.

Efar relaxed and shifted back to human. He wouldn't waste time dressing when he'd be flying again soon. Still naked, he stepped around fallen mercenaries and approached Captain. "Thank you, my friend, for joining in the fight with me. Now I need you to go help Marie." He pointed in the direction Gwen had gone.

The horse violently shook his head, ears slanted back in negation. He swung his head at his back.

"Fiera sent you, didn't she? She wants you to show me where he's taking her. But, I already know he'll fly her back to his father's castle. I'll be flying, so you won't be able to keep up. Marie needs protection. Now, go. Tell Fiera I'm right behind them."

The horse reared, pivoting on his haunches. He bolted toward Gwen's house.

Efar changed once more into his weary griffin and climbed into the dark night, following Fiera and the Royal Dragon Prince Bartheleme.

****

Fiera squirmed in the grip of the giant dragon. Cool night air ripped past her in waves every time the beast flapped its wings. They skimmed inches above the dark points of living trees. She was sure she could reach down and touch them. The ominous black shapes of mountains loomed on the horizon. There was no other creature to share the moon and stars with them.

Fiera, can you still hear me? It was Captain.

Yes, but I don't know for how much longer.

We defeated the soldiers. You should have seen me! The first man swung his sword at me, but I kicked him hard in the stomach and he fell to the ground vomiting. I think I might have nicked his ribs. Maybe broken one or two of them. The next man raised his bow, aiming at Efar, but I was behind him. I reared and—

126

Captain! Focus.

After a second's hesitation, he continued, sullen notes in his 'voice'. *Efar is flying after you. He says he knows where you're going. He sent me to protect Marie.*

Marie has been captured already. She's a prisoner of this dragon man, too!

No. She's here. I've seen her. She's safe.

Safe? She wanted to cry with the relief that flooded over her. Then, the white-hot poker of anger she'd pushed down inside since being abducted forced its way to the surface. She'd been tricked into betraying her friends. Tricked by this man who now held her captive.

Dragon, can you still hear me?

Why wouldn't I?

I can only speak to animals in my mind.

You spoke to me as a man.

Yes, but I've never been able to speak to shifters before. Why now? Why you?

The dragon was silent. She squirmed again, trying to rearrange her ribs over the dragon's knuckle, but to no avail. She sighed. There would be bruises. She looked up at the moon, her heart seething at her helplessness. In that moment, a shadow in the shape of a large bird crossed the face of the moon.

Efar had caught up to them.

Might I at least ride on top, Dragon? We're too high for me to escape. If I try, I would fall to my death.

The dragon's response was to tighten its talons around her body. The knuckle that had been offending her ribs slid across her back to dig into a new place on her other side.

You're hurting me. Or do you intend to deliver me as a corpse?

The only sound was the heavy *whup* of the wings and the soft low moan as they moved up and down through the air.

At least, tell me why you want me.

When the dragon still didn't answer, she sighed, seething over her predicament. She stared up at Efar. There had to be something she could do to help him. She couldn't change the living cells of the dragon, but, if the talons, which were dead cells, were in the right place, she could change those into something else. She squirmed once more, hoping the dragon would reposition its grip again.

Above her, Efar folded back his wings, tucked his head, and dove toward them.

****

Efar twisted his dive toward the dragon below, as if he could drill right through the giant beast. That's what he wanted to do; it had Fiera.

He would rip that monster apart for stealing her from him. All the world knew there was nothing as fierce as a wronged griffin. And *this* griffin had been *very* wronged. Fury lit across his body in a keen, knife-edged determination to free her. It added fuel to his dive, tightening his body into a slim projectile striking from above like lightning from Thor's hammer. The wind whistled past him, his eyes teared from his speed, and his vision blurred.

In glimpses between flaps of the giant beast's wings, he saw Fiera fighting in the dragon's clutches, struggling to reach the hard nail of the talon. He saw her plan immediately—she hoped to free herself by changing the dead cells into something malleable.

Then she'd fall.

And he'd better be there to catch her.

He was almost on the dragon, a mere dozen feet away, when it turned, laying back on the night wind

128

currents so that its wings and belly, with Fiera hugged tightly against it, faced the moon. A belch of fire erupted from its mouth, blinding in the night. Somehow, somewhere, it had found brimstone.

Efar's speed made it impossible to stop. He tightened his corkscrew and used the shift it caused in his pattern to veer off to the right. The move wasn't quite quick enough and Efar found himself flying through a sea of fire and sparks. A shock of pain seared across the left side of this body, and the air stank of brimstone, seared skin, and burnt feathers.

The sudden loss of feathers on Efar's left wing meant he had no way to stabilize himself. The power dive that was meant to hammer the dragon drove Efar toward the ground. He did his best to slow and to angle his path so landing wouldn't be so disastrous, but there was so little time.

Tree branches reached out to snag him, tearing the skin he had left, not helping him slow much. He slammed into the ground with a jarring crash, the cracks and pops of breaking bones and tearing ligaments loud in his ears.

As a rain of leaves and twigs fell down on him, in the brief split-second before he lost consciousness, he saw the dragon right itself, Fiera frantically scrambling for its talon.

He spoke a quiet prayer in her direction. "Please. No. Not now. I can't catch you."

Then it all went black.

****

Fiera stared down into the dark forest below. She could barely make out the pale form of the griffin, surrounded by broken branches and leaves as if in a nest.

Her heart stopped. Efar wasn't moving.

Frantically, she resumed her scramble for the dragon's talon. She wasn't sure what she could turn it into that would make the creature let go of her. Something sharp, perhaps, so it would open its claw. If she could reach it. Leaning so far that her ribs dug against the dragon's knuckle and stretching her arm as far as she could still made the talon a good six inches away.

Captain, can you hear me? She held her breath, hoping the distance between them wasn't too great. *Captain?*

When there was no answer from the horse, unbidden tears welled up. Efar was alone now. There was no one to help him.

Savagely, she wiped the tears away. No. She would not cry!

There had been no tears all those years locked away in her parents' home. There would be no tears now. Not when she'd done the things she had for love. The blame didn't belong to her. It belonged to the foul beast clutching her. Somehow, some way, she'd make him pay for what he'd done.

The reptilian stench of the dragon filled her nostrils as she once again searched the trees below her. There had to be some animal nearby! Spying a group of bats flitting among the dark branches, she singled out a large one. *You are a magnificent looking bat. I bet you fly far and fast.*

Far and fast. The voice was high and hollow in Fiera's head. It flew close, beating its wings frantically to keep up with the larger winged creature that held her, shying away each time the giant wings came close.

Might I trouble you for a favor? There's a man-bird who's fallen just over there. She pointed, not sure if the bat could pick up the gesture.

Man-bird who's fallen. It darted back and forth,

130

dodging between dragon wing thrusts, working its way closer to her.

He needs help from a friend in Chester. She gave a description of Gwen's barn and house. *The man-bird needs help right away or he may die. Friend in Chester. Right away.*

It didn't leave.

Did the bat understand her? Or was it echoing her? *Please help us. I'd like to think that if you're ever in need of help, someone will help you.*

For a moment all was silent except the wind moaning as the dragon's wing cut through it. Then the bat took off in the direction of Chester, leaving this thought in her head: *Friend in Chester.*

She closed her eyes in silent thanks and whispered, "Hurry."

As the dragon winged westward, the trees changed to fields and then hills. It breached the edge of the mountains and began to climb higher into the cool night air. The sun was rising in the east, behind them, and it cast a pink glow across the peaks.

A bone deep shiver settled into Fiera. She tried to still herself, but to no avail. The dragon, perhaps noticing her discomfort, tucked its claws close against its body. Held tight against the reptilian skin, the stench was nearly overwhelming. Yet, unlike other reptiles, the skin was warm as she huddled against it. *What is your name? Efar knows you. Who are you?*

The dragon hesitated before it answered. *I am Prince Bartheleme, son of King Cynan The Mighty.*

Fiera sucked in her breath. Captured by royalty. She seemed to be in bigger trouble than she thought. *Why do you want me?*

This time the dragon didn't answer. As they climbed even higher to crest the last of the peaks, the shiver that had been driven out of Fiera by the warmth

131

of the dragon took over again.

Without hesitation, the dragon rolled its neck so that it could face her. It opened its mouth and threw out a small stream of fire far enough below her so she didn't burn. The sulfurous heat enveloped her and her chill immediately melted away.

If the Prince was going to kill her, why see to her comfort? He was making a mistake keeping her alive. Wherever he took her, she'd find a way to escape. And if Efar were dead, she'd come back to the land of dragons for revenge.

****

Bartheleme landed at the gates proper to his father's castle, setting down the woman. He stalked to the edge of the catwalk and belched out the remains of his fire. If he shifted to human with the white brimstone in his stomach, he'd be sick. He'd actually seen a few dragon shifters die from careless management of their fires.

When he'd finished purging it all, he took the robe offered by one of the royal guards and shifted to human, shrinking in size, becoming...less. He hated the human form, but so much of the court business had to be conducted that way. If they all remained dragons, there would be no room. The second closest secret was the sheer number of dragon shifters. Their number was rival to any army.

Donning the robe, a deep royal purple with gold trim, he turned toward the other two guards, appraising the woman he'd captured, Fiera. She stood defiantly, a few feet away, her back to the guards, studying the castle. Her arms hung limply at her sides, but her hands were curled into fists.

Bartheleme cleared his throat to get her attention. When Fiera turned to him, her face looked as if a

132

thundercloud had descended upon it. Her brows were knit close together, overshadowing her narrowed eyes. Her chin was jutted forward and her jaw was clenched tight.

She didn't look like the others: cowed and afraid, he thought. Not even the men. No, she in fact looked quite determined...and livid. She would bear watching.

He pivoted on his heel and led the group into the castle, the tails of his robe bouncing against his legs and his bare feet slapping on the cobblestone. Not altogether dignified. He hated the human form.

****

Between the guards, Fiera followed the royal prince into the castle. More guards dressed in white finery lined the halls and stood outside rooms. The walls were a gray stone with rich tapestries. Wide torch-dotted passages led off to the right and left. The first passage was narrow and close to the outer walls; it would be for the guards. She began counting the hallways as they passed. She planned to escape and didn't want to get lost.

The vaulted ceilings fascinated her. Though she'd never been in a castle before, she doubted other castles entertained ceilings so high. But then, considering the occupants, they made sense.

The Prince, not looking back, motioned toward a long stretch of a hallway to the right.

Immediately, the guards gripped Fiera's arms and turned her into the indicated passage. The floor was at an upward slant and, about halfway up, they rudely shoved her though a doorway. When she turned to berate the guards for their roughness, the door slammed in her face, followed by the sound of a bar sliding across it.

Frowning, she turned to see what kind of prison she'd been locked into, only to find herself pleasantly surprised. Instead of dingy grey walls with tiny barred windows and a rag on the floor for a bed, the room was bright and richly furnished. The bed was large and spacious, with deep blankets, a heavy mattress, and a canopy. Thick rugs adorned the floor. And an empty fireplace filled one whole wall.

Seven slits of open windows adorned the walls, letting sunlight flood into the room and it was to these that Fiera rushed. They were barely wide enough for her to stick her head through and she twisted sideways to wriggle her shoulders through as well, leaning far out to inspect her chances of escape. The outer walls fell away sharply to a wide moat below. Her room was probably a good hundred feet above the ground. Below her, more window slits dotted the castle. In fact, all around her there were nothing but slits.

For a moment she couldn't understand the reason for the narrow windows, but then it dawned on her that she was now in a land of flying shapeshifters. The shape of the windows kept everyone out.

From the room behind her came a rasping sound and she pulled back inside, turning to see the door open to admit an elderly woman who bustled over to the fireplace.

Fiera eyed the open door, but the white uniformed guards glaring at her with sharp swords unsheathed quelled any desire she had to try an immediate escape. She turned her attention to the woman squatting in front of the fireplace. Her clothes were clean and neat. Though her whole body shook with the movements of starting a fire, she didn't seem to be malnourished nor sickly. What was visible of her arms showed a fair amount of muscle. When the woman stood and turned around, Fiera discovered that what she'd

134

originally assumed were age wrinkles were actually long jagged scars across her face.

Fiera startled, inadvertently stepping back. The woman ducked her head, blushing and mumbling apologies for her disturbance. She made to rush past and out of the room, but Fiera grabbed her arm. "You have no reason for apologies. It's I who should apologize to you."

The woman hesitated and then curtsied, her head still bowed. "Not necessary, Miss. But I thank you. If you need anything, send a guard for Maybelle."

"Who did this to you, Maybelle?" Fiera blurted, not letting go of the woman. She had to find out what kind of trouble she could expect. "Was it the master of this castle?"

The woman lifted her head, her face lit with surprise. The scars pulled and stretched her face into a mask of horror. "The King? Never! He's been good to me. Took me in when none other would. I really must get about my duties."

Fiera let her go and sat on the bed, staring at the fledgling fire. Nothing was as she'd expected. After being hunted by the fat man for days, then being tricked and forcibly brought to this land of dragons, she expected harsh treatment and a dungeon prison. True, there were guards to keep her locked away, but her accommodations spoke more of a guest than a prisoner. Also, those very same guards were dressed in clean white uniforms. Neither they, nor the maid, had smelled of brew or body sweat. They were well cared for and respected their master.

She flopped back on the bed and stared at the canopy. Nothing made sense.

****

Efar, still as a griffin, slowly woke in the arid heat of midafternoon. His whole body hurt, as if being rolled over by a giant boulder. The most pronounced was a deep ache in his left leg that rolled his stomach. Probably broken. His left collarbone, too. Beneath him, against the ground, his left side stung as only a fresh burn could.

He struggled to his feet, keeping most of his weight on his right side. During his slow return to upright, he discovered one or two broken ribs as well as something that pinched in his wing every time he moved it. The broken ends of the bones in his leg ground together as he moved. He could immobilize any broken bones. Real birds had fused collarbones anyway. It was the burn that worried him; if he'd lost too many feathers, he wouldn't be able to fly for a very long time. It would take much longer to reach Fiera.

The effort of being fully upright on injured limbs sent shocks of pain curling throughout him and was almost more than he could stand. He craned his neck and lifted his wing, wincing at the white-hot lance of pain that shot through him and inspecting the damage to his left side. From mid-thigh through his underarm and up under his wing was charred black with giant, angry red blisters raised around the edges. In the center of the black was what looked like a thick braid of leather. He'd never seen a burn so bad. It would leave a scar. Strange it didn't hurt except at the very edges.

As far as his feathers went, it was hard to tell which were actually burnt to brittleness and which were still usable.

Bark snapped in the underbrush behind him, and he pivoted on his right front eagle's claw, staggering, neck stretched and wings spread in aggression, hissing and clacking his beak.

Captain's long equine nose poked through the

leaves, blowing hard. Then the rest of his body followed, accompanied by Marie and Gwen. A short fellow came last, leading two more horses.

Efar sank to the ground in relief as he shifted to human. Marie unfolded a blanket and covered his hips. The pain from his broken bones echoed all the way to his fingertips and toes. His stomach rolled violently. Through clenched teeth, he asked Gwen, "How did you find me?"

"We were all packed and ready to leave as you instructed, but a bat appeared. It flew right up to us, then flitted away, always in the same direction. After a few times, he," she paused in her task of making a prayer circle around him and pointed to Captain, "started walking after it and we followed."

Walking? Efar frowned. "How long ago was that?"

"Yesterday morning. Once we realized the bat was probably sent by Fiera, we picked up the pace."

While the short man tended the two horses, Captain wandered nearby in the woods, grazing and waiting his turn. Marie squatted beside Efar, laying a large leaf on the ground in front of her and flipping open the pouch she kept tied at her waist.

Opening two small packets, Marie poured the whole of the powdered contents together on the leaf. After a brief hesitation, she pulled out another packet and added its contents as well. She stirred the powders together with her finger and then handed the leaf to him, pantomiming what he was to do.

His tongue numbed the very second he licked the bitter mix. Potent stuff. He'd need it. Finishing off the painkiller, he lay back so that his injured left side was facing up. Euphoria settled over him as Marie cleaned and doctored his burns. Gwen's chanting soothed Efar's anxieties. His eyelids grew heavy.

Snapping his eyes open, he tried to rouse himself to wakefulness. He didn't need to sleep. Fiera needed his help. The fog that had descended over him refused to leave and his body no longer obeyed his commands. Gwen's words became nothing but garbled nonsense from a great distance.

His last thought before drifting off to sleep was how Marie had betrayed him by putting a sleeping agent in the painkiller.

****

Fiera squeezed her head out the narrow slit of a window and surveyed her handiwork. The once smooth stone castle wall below her was now adorned to halfway down with thin ledges and tiny hand holds. The rising sun cast long shadows of the steps across the face of the stone. She glanced around the castle grounds It would be easy to spot her work in this light.

It had been over twenty-four hours since she'd been brought as a captive to the land of the dragons. During that time, no one had visited her except Maybelle, who silently brought her plates of delicate food, tended the fire, and quickly retreated.

Not that Fiera minded; it gave her plenty of time to work on her escape.

At first, she'd thought to trick her guards into leaving with a horde of rodents, but the castle seemed strangely devoid of mice and rats. Her next idea was to magic a hole in one of the walls or the floor, but not knowing what, or who, was on the other side had quickly led her to dismiss that idea.

That left her with a window that was too high off the ground to let her jump safely. Hence the stairs. It had been slow progress, forging steps the right distance apart. She'd had to widen the stone window, climb out and test each ledge. The first ones were so narrow that she slipped off and, if not for the handholds she'd had the foresight to make, she would have fallen to her death on the boulders that bordered the moat.

She wished to just climb out the window and stay perched on each ledge as she made the next, but she felt sure someone would either notice her absence from captivity or spot her clinging to the side of the castle. Instead, after each step was made and tested, she'd had to climb back into her prison and narrow the window again before she could make the next rung in her escape ladder. It was truly exhausting work, but she pushed her magic on and on.

Fiera yawned, shaking with the fierceness of it. She eyed the bed, but then turned back to the window, ignoring the tray of food. She wouldn't rest until she was well away from this place. Until she was safe by Efar's side. He just had to be okay. Their relationship couldn't end there.

****

When Efar woke again, the sky was in its last throes of sunset. Brilliant hues of yellow, orange, and purple covered the clouds in ripples, washing the leaves in the trees with a gentle golden light.

Marie lay sleeping, curled up beside him, still within the circle Gwen had built. Candles sat atop mounds of fresh earth in the four directions all around him. Outside the circle, Gwen and her male friend were talking quietly by a small campfire, a huge pile of tree leaves beside them.

Efar gently shifted his leg beneath the blanket, testing the break. Immediately, Marie was up and beside him, frowning and lifting the blanket to check his injuries.

Gwen stood and walked toward him, carefully stopping outside the healing circle.

With gritted teeth, he asked the tall witch, "How long this time?"

"Since yesterday. You needed it." She motioned to Marie. "She's a good nurse, but she's still healing from her own injuries. That's why I left her inside with you."

As Gwen began walking the perimeter of the circle, softly praying, Efar turned his attention to Marie. She was a smart one. And yes, he had needed the rest. But now he needed to get moving again. He smiled down at the girl, his heart swelling with how fond he'd become of her. "Well, Nurse, am I fit for travel now?"

The girl scowled and violently shook her head, pointing at the bindings that held his bones in place.

Efar said, "I understand it's broken, but that won't really stop me from going after Fiera, will it?"

She bit her lip and rocked back on her heels.

Gwen said, "Your collar bone will keep you from flying. You'll have to ride Captain."

Efar growled to himself and shook his head. "There's no time."

The short man joined the group. "I rather thought you'd say that. I have an idea."

"And you are...?"

"Laurence. I assist Gwen." He motioned to Gwen and the circle.

"How about you tell me your idea while I figure out how to stand." Efar bunched the blanket around his hips and reached his right hand toward Marie for help.

She crossed her arms and looked away, a dark scowl once again covering her face.

He sighed and gently said, "You understand Fiera's in trouble, right? I'm the only one who can get to her in time to save her."

"As much as I hate to admit it, he's right." Gwen, finished with her prayers, stepped within the confines of the circle, the male witch right behind her. While the tall witch took Efar's outstretched hand, Laurence clamped Efar's left arm against his fractured ribs and lifted from behind.

Once up, it took a moment for Efar to steady himself with most of his weight on his right leg. The ache deep in his left leg was nothing compared to the excruciating spike of pain in his ribcage whenever he breathed too deeply. The left side of his collarbone had a dull throb in it as well, but he'd yet to feel anything from the burn that covered his side.

He hobbled toward the campfire with Gwen's and the short man's help, wincing with every step. Marie followed. He said to Laurence, "Suppose you tell me your plan."

****

Bartheleme lounged in his chair while a servant distributed roast potatoes onto his plate beside the game hen. His twin, the royal princess Cecily, sat across from Bartheleme, impatiently waiting her turn. When her food arrived, she dug in with gusto; she was no delicate flower.

Guards entered the room at the far end, escorting Fiera. Her hair stuck out in all different directions with giant knots in it; dark circles underscored her eyes; and she shuffled with the lifeless dull gait only the exhausted shared. It had been nearly thirty-six hours since he'd brought her to the castle and it didn't look as if she'd slept any of it.

The guards stopped her beside his sister at an empty place setting.

"I'm King Cynan. But, I suspect you already know that." The king stood and walked over to Fiera. Without waiting for a response from her, he continued, "Your maid, Maybelle, tells me you aren't eating. Is this true?"

This time he waited for a response, but when met with only a bitter pursing of her lips, he took the chair and pulled it out from the table. "Sit."

With narrowed suspicious eyes, she lowered into the chair. While the king returned to his place at the head of the table, servants rushed to fill Fiera's plate with steaming meat and potatoes. As they finished, the King motioned to her food. "Eat."

When Fiera made no move to comply, he sighed and said, "Eat. Please. We're not your enemies."

With that, Fiera's bitter expression turned dark. "Am I not your prisoner?" She looked directly at Bartheleme.

He smiled back, picking through his food. He would not be baited by her.

The king shook his head. "You're a guest."

"With guards?" She raised her eyebrows.

He lifted his hands to ward off her anger. "Only temporarily."

Bartheleme watched the solid ridge of her jaw turn hard. He could tell already the way this would go. His appetite suddenly lost, he pushed his plate away. A servant sprang forward and cleared it from his sight. Another servant offered a sweet, but he waved that away, too, instead holding up his half-empty cup of mead. It was immediately filled.

He settled back in his chair and watched as the inevitable events unfolded. Glancing at his sister, he saw she knew how the conversation would turn as well as he, but she continued eating, though slower. Of the three of them, only their father, the king, seemed oblivious of what was to come.

Fiera said nothing. She neither ate nor drank. She stared at the king as if willing him to finish his half of the tragedy.

****

Fiera glared at King Cynan. Between them sat a woman Fiera could only assume was the princess, judging by how similar she appeared to Prince Bartheleme: same dark hair, same sculpted cheeks, same intent gaze, though hers was focused on the full spoon she lifted to her mouth in a regular rhythm.

Across the table, the prince watched Fiera with narrowed eyes and a wry twist to his mouth.

The king's voice filled Fiera's head. *The guards will be removed as soon as you agree to our terms.*

She continued her glare. The first time a human, Prince Bartheleme, had spoken in her mind, she'd been caught unaware and had given herself away. Not so this time; she gave no indication she'd heard.

The king sighed again and set down his utensil. *My son has never lied to me and he wouldn't start with something as trifling as you. He tells me you can hear our thoughts and I believe him.*

Across the table, the prince's wry smile turned to a smirk.

"Why have you kidnapped me?" Her spoken words rang harshly off the stone walls, ineloquent after the king's smooth voice in her head.

King Cynan dabbed his fingers in a bowl of water and wiped them on a towel offered by a servant. "Because you can hear our thoughts."

"You kidnap everyone who can read your minds?"

He nodded his grey-haired head. "Yes. Then they decide to live here the rest of their lives. We give them coin, clothing, food, work, a home, and land if they wish."

"And if they decide to leave?"

"It's a good life here. People are happy."

143

She gritted her teeth. Why wouldn't he answer? "Do any leave?"

"None."

"I have been a prisoner all my life. Just because it's a bigger, kinder type of cell doesn't mean it isn't one."

"The choice is yours. You may certainly choose not to stay."

There was something in the way he said it that made Fiera take notice. "You'll just let me leave?"

"No. We cannot allow someone with your knowledge of us to go back into the world."

The prince sat up in his chair and leaned across the table toward her. "If you leave, it will mean your death."

Fiera supposed any rational person would be terrified at the prospect of being killed, but it only stoked the rage within her. She leaned in toward him and spat out the words. "I will not be forced to stay. I choose death!"

The princess finally looked up. The king opened his mouth to speak again, but she put her hand on his arm, staying his words. She met Fiera's gaze. "None here seek your death. We'll bring anyone here that you wish, even your griffin lover. You must live somewhere. Why not here? Please reconsider."

More than anything, Fiera wanted to please this woman, perhaps even befriend her, but staying captive in the land of dragons was something she couldn't do. She slowly relaxed against the back of her chair and calmly said, "I choose death."

Across from her, Prince Bartheleme didn't seem surprised. He settled back in his chair again and nodded once to the guards behind her.

Rough hands lifted her from the chair.

****

Efar found a break in the north-south mountain ridges and cut through it to the west, saving himself a good deal of flying instead of going around the seaward end of the range. High peaks rose on either side of him. If it hadn't been so close to dragon territory, his people would have made their home there, instead of the mountains to the southeast.

A leaf ripped loose from his wing, exposing a hole that sent him into a graceless wobble until he figured out how to compensate. It was the sixth leaf he'd lost from those that he, Laurence, and Gwen had woven among his singed feathers. At first, he hadn't been sure he'd be able to fly with the one-sided weight of the vegetation, but after a few attempts, he'd finally gotten managed it.

His left arm, now as a griffin's claw, was in a sling, to help protect his collarbone from the dangling weight. Marie had splinted his leg tightly, knowing that limb would be sacrificed when he landed.

As he rounded the last abutment of rock, he curved south toward his destination, arcing away from the leading range, toward the lowlands. Dawn was stretching across the horizon, painting everything in either golden glow or blue shadow. His own shadow flitted across the various farms and holdings below.

He turned toward the only castle in the region: that of King Cynan and his twin children, Bartheleme and Cecily. Efar doubted the king would just hand over Fiera. It may take threats. He needed to find her first. And he needed to plan his escape strategy. Just in case the only way to rescue her was to steal her back.

Another leaf tore loose, causing a cavalcade of leaves to exit their moorings. He wobbled helplessly, aiming for a plot of soft clover.

With a grunt, he landed, trying to put most of his weight on his good right lion's leg. Still, some of his weight caught on his broken left leg and, even though the splint held well, a spire of pain lanced all the way throughout his leg to his hip, sending his stomach into roiling spasms. He hissed through his beak, the sound loud in the empty field.

Efar balanced himself and as he slowly changed back to human, his bandages, splint and the woven leaves sloughed to the ground.

Once the change was completed, he re-splinted his leg and retied the sling for his left arm. Though it was a smaller and lighter weight limb than the griffin's, it still hung heavy on a smaller collarbone.

His next order of business being to find clothes, he hobbled toward the castle, watching for anything to wear. In the land of shapeshifters, nakedness was nothing unusual, not even stare-worthy, and spare clothes were easy to come by.

His own people, when they took to their animal selves, hid their clothes under rocks, in stumps, anywhere but in plain sight. Here, however, the closer he came to the center of town, the more piles of clothes he found on the street corners. In no time at all, he located something in his size. Complete with boots only a tiny bit big.

At the castle gate, he was stopped by an honor guard of four men dressed in white. They glared at him belligerently and at least two sniffed the air at his foreign animal odor. One, a beefy fellow with a scar across one brow ground out, "What do you want here, Griffin?"

"I have business with the king." Efar met the guards' glares with one of his own. On the pyramid of life, griffins and dragons were par.

The stare-down lasted a few more seconds, and

146

then Scar-face recognized him, gave a small bow, and sent one of his men with a message to the court. Within minutes, the messenger returned and Efar was escorted into the throne room.

The castle was rich with thick tapestries and rugs, high ceilings, and ornately carved furniture sitting heavily against walls that held golden sconces. Flickering candlelight danced across a marble floor. The old king, seated dead center of the room in his giant bejeweled throne, watched with measuring eyes as Efar approached.

Efar struggled against his splint, dropping to one knee, bowing his head. "King Cynan."

"She is no longer here." The king's voice was gravelly, ancient. No one knew for certain the monarch's age. He seemed to have been king forever. It was remarkable he only had two children to show for all his time on Earth. What was even more remarkable was that he'd not been slaughtered by those seeking his crown, including, but not limited to, his son. It spoke toward his strength as a ruler.

"Sire?" Efar kept on one knee, his gaze on the floor.

"My son has sent her away. I know not where."

Efar waited for more, but after a few seconds, someone tapped him on the shoulder and he looked up into a thick face with a scarred brow. The throne was empty. Getting to his feet proved to be nearly impossible and, in the end, Scar-face, smirking, had to help him.

Once free of the castle, Efar hobbled to a hillside heavy with low-hanging trees. He harvested a large pile of leaves, grew in his griffin wings and started weaving in the greenery. Occasionally, he checked for anyone approaching. Griffins weren't exactly welcome there, and though he'd been safe enough under the banner of the dragon king, the open countryside was a different matter.

Glancing at the castle, he noticed the thin outline of steps part way down one otherwise smooth back wall. He stared at it, trying to puzzle out why the dragons would have built that, but could come up with no logical conclusion. That left only one other explanation: built on the far side of the castle, the steps had to be an aborted escape attempt. Perhaps formed with magic by a certain witch he was hunting.

With a satisfied grunt, Efar turned back to the task of weaving leaves amongst the burnt feathers of his left wing. At least he knew Fiera *had* been there.

****

Fiera chuckled at her good fortune, though because of her extreme exhaustion, her giggle came out more as a maniacal cackle. Not that it mattered; there was no one near to hear her. What mattered was that, instead of taking her back to her previous room, the guards brought her to a holding cell in the deep dark dungeon.

They'd locked her prison door and left her alone to await her death. Perhaps they thought she'd change her mind once she had time to think on her choice. Either way, that was a good thing. Alone, she could now work her magic and escape here much more easily than from the tower room. True, she still couldn't just open a hole in the side of the castle and walk out; she was relatively sure she was too far below ground for that, but at least she didn't have to work on the slow forming stone ladder any longer.

She'd be ready when Efar came for her. And he would come. She knew it.

Glad she'd paid attention to the castle's layout, she rubbed her hands together and placed them on the cell door, willing her magic to rearrange the structure of the wood. There was no welling up inside her, no river of force flowing through her. Not even her fingers tingled.

Fiera sputtered her lips in frustration and concentrated. She'd had no sleep for thirty-six hours and had eaten very little. She'd overworked her magic, pushing it far beyond normal usages and she'd not had enough training, nor time, with Gwen to know how to replenish it on her own. Still, there had to be some small dregs left.

She closed her eyes, cutting out her surroundings, narrowing her focus on the door beneath her fingers, using every part of her will to call forth that which was in her. Slowly, her fingers began to prick with the telltale sign her magic was working. The door shifted incrementally beneath her hands. The hole she formed was thin and barely big enough for her to slip through. It was jagged as if torn naturally from rotten wood. She had to keep her abilities hidden as much as possible. It was bad enough the dragons knew she could read their minds.

Squeezing through the hole with a satisfied grin, Fiera crept back the way she'd been brought, upward toward the main prison exit. Once at the door, she rose onto her tiptoes to peer through the barred window at the top. A guard in white finery stood no more than two feet away, his back to her. Lowering herself out of view, she leaned against the wall and considered her options.

She still wasn't high enough in the castle for an escape directly out the side. Her only other way to go was right out this door. There was just enough room behind the guard for her to slip out, but then what? She couldn't stand behind the guard all day.

Feet scuffed outside and Fiera whirled away in panic as a key sounded in the lock. She stared down the long string of cell doors and dashed to the closest. Her hands slipped on the latch, but then found it and she flung the door open, dashing inside and pulling the door shut behind her. The cell was empty, completely devoid of anything. Huddling in the corner, she placed her hands on the wall on either side and concentrated, forcing the weak remnants of her magic to her will.

Footsteps sounded in the corridor, walking down the narrow hallway toward her original cell. Even as the walls around her bent to her will and slowly moved to cover her, a bellow of fury echoed through the prison. Running feet of guards passed her hiding place. Cell doors started slamming open along the corridor, working toward her.

Fiera bit her lip hard. The salt of her blood filled her mouth as the pain exploded her magic into the moving walls under her hands. Her work didn't have to be good; it just had to pass the inspection of a brief glance.

****

In a rage, Bartheleme followed his men down the corridor, checking the cells they'd already looked in. Without fail, those that were supposed to be empty were, and those with occupants were still locked.

How had the girl escaped them? The door where she'd been held was obviously rotted and enabled her leaving, but where had she gone after that? The guards hadn't seen her leave the prison and he believed them. Down to a man, there wasn't a single guard that didn't respect his wrath.

The girl's cell was halfway down the corridor. If she hadn't come this direction, perhaps she'd gone the other. Bartheleme left the last cell he'd checked and walked back down the corridor, pausing at Fiera's cell. He stared at the jagged hole, then he bent and took a closer look. The wood looked rotten, but something wasn't right. The edges were a bit smoother than they should have been. Even the sharp points were slightly rounded.

So, not broken. The boards had apparently been formed that way. By a witch. One that didn't want to hurt herself escaping. He stood and frowned. Why was the hole so small when she could have made it much bigger?

He pictured how she'd looked the last time he'd seen her, disheveled and exhausted. Sudden understanding hit him with the obvious answer—because for whatever reason, Fiera couldn't make the hole bigger.

Slowly, he pivoted on his heel and gazed back up the corridor toward the prison exit. With limited abilities, there was really only one direction she would have gone.

In silence, he rechecked each cell, his men clustered and following, watching. He found what he was looking for in the cell closest to the exit. One corner was misshapen with a supporting stone foot that jutted into the room. It was barely big enough to hide a girl Fiera's size.

Taking the nearest guard's sword, he raised it high above his head and brought it down sharply on the stone with a loud crack. The stone crumbled and beneath it cowered the red-haired girl.

With a satisfied smile, Bartheleme stepped back to let his men apprehend their prisoner.

Chapter 8

Efar studied the castle as he flew past in the dark. He banked and flew by again, closer, taking care not to go too far around where the guards could see him. Slowly, he approached the slices of a ladder formed in the side of the tower, inhaling deeply, filling his griffin's nose with the stench of dragon. But mixed among that were unmistakable traces of Fiera's unique spicy-woodsy scent.

She'd been here.

She'd created the steps from the stone of the castle, but had ended them while still too high to jump safely. She must have been interrupted.

He circled upward to the window, peeking in with his creature's eagle sight, but the room was empty and, sniffing, he judged it had been for a few hours.

Where was she? Was it as the old king had said, that Bartheleme had taken her away?

As if thinking on his nemesis brought him to sight, the giant dragon shapeshifter rose from around the front of the castle below, Fiera squirming in his claws. Three more dragons followed.

Efar cut sharply, moving in close to the stone wall. He flew in silence, angling up and back the direction from which Bartheleme's party had come. If he could just get behind them, remain invisible to those below, and not be discovered by the invariable guards in the turrets above, he'd have it made. Not a problem.

Almost immediately upon that thought, a leaf he'd woven within his damaged wing feathers worked loose at one end, undulating loudly in the air currents. He plucked the offending leaf out with his beak and held his breath, hoping the wind had carried the noise away from...everyone.

A small dragon at the back of the group cocked its head and slowly circled out of formation, letting the air currents carry it higher, searching left and right for the cause of the buzzing. It would be no time before it smelled the intruding griffin.

Efar tucked his wings and plummeted, dropping past the tail of the dragon. Once he was low enough the air current wouldn't be as noticeable, he opened his wings again and thrust as hard as he could, hoping another leaf wouldn't give him away, shooting across the front of the castle merely a dozen feet above the heads of the guard. As he reached the sanctuary of the far side, he glanced back.

Neither of the guards had noticed him. The searching dragon had given up and rejoined the group.

Efar circled the castle, keeping low and to the gloomy night shadows. He came up well behind the Prince and his party and followed them.

Ahead, the writhing form in the lead dragon's clutches ceased movement briefly, then resumed with added ferocity.

Fiera had seen him.

****

153

Fiera struggled against the tight claws that bound her high above the earth. At the same time, she watched the distant pale speck floating in the dark behind the last dragon in Bartheleme's retinue. Could it be Efar? It had to be.

Her heart surged with hope. He'd found her. He was here.

She renewed her struggle with the giant beast who held her captive. If she could have used her magic on a living creature, she would have used it now. But she couldn't and her magic was all played out. She called out in her mind to any nearby animals, excluding the dragons from her pleas, but the drought had kept the hills and forest below bare and made most critters scarce. It would be many years before that part of the country recovered and was once again teeming with life. Though she reached as far as she could with her mind, only one or two birds answered. What could a couple birds do against four dragons?

Her captors carried her north, higher now, against the cool of the night sky, mindless of her efforts to free herself. They were apparently also unaware of the griffin, close behind now, flying near to the ground, weaving among the bare tree trunks.

Eventually, the air filled with the salt of sea water. Just as the sound of crashing waves became audible to her, Bartheleme swooped low and, as he passed, he dumped Fiera on a rock ledge that overlooked the sea. He flew out, over the water, a dark monster hidden in the dark sky.

She scrambled to her feet and, though she didn't have the eyesight of either the griffin or the dragons, stared out at the black sea. Up close, water rushed toward her in huge growling curls, cascading over each other, to shatter upon the base of her ledge, sending spray high above to soak her, though only a few drops reached her. It had to be high tide for it to be so far up the cliffside in non-drought times.

To her left, a fingernail slice of a moon hung cleanly over the distant flat expanse of sea. The moon's light trailed a faint path in water that seemed to go on forever. Off to the other side of her, the sea was bordered by a dark landmass that loomed menacingly in the night.

The three small dragons, two brown and one yellow, landed beside her. They crowded against her, pushing her back against the cliff wall. One of the browns clamped heavy irons around her wrists with its dexterous claws. A thick chain ran from the wrist cuffs to the rock wall, disappearing deep within, an ancient sacrificial spot to appease the sea gods.

No way was she getting loose without her magic. Even Efar couldn't break the iron loops. She groaned at the uselessness of wasting her magic on the stone steps earlier. If only she'd known she'd need it now.

Out in the darkness, over the sea, a ball of flame exploded into being. The three guards moved well back from her, still in dragon form.

A shiver coursed through Fiera. Bartheleme meant to burn her alive.

****

Bartheleme reveled in the smell of the brimstone mixed with the cool sea air. He swooped low in the night, sheering the plane of water, briefly skimming just below the surface, the liquid rolling over his reptilian skin like satin.

Lifting above the sea, he curled toward shore, water sheeting off him as rain. He speculatively eyed the cliffside and its stoic captive. This was Fiera's last chance. If she begged for mercy, said even one word that might lead to an agreement of the king's terms, he would let her live.

Otherwise, he would burn her alive.

He again curved away from her, showing his profile, so she would get a full view of what was coming.

Then he sent a long curl of flame into the night.

****

Efar smelled the sea long before he reached it. That worried him more than anything. What did Bartheleme have planned? Was he going to take Fiera far out to sea and drown her? He didn't know if she could swim, but he doubted it.

Putting on the speed, he fanned his wings wide to push harder, coming up out of the trees. The time for hiding was over.

He crested the ridge just as Bartheleme sent a plume of fire over the water. Even from this distance, though, Efar could see that the dragon's claws were empty. He'd dropped her into the water already.

Like an arrow, he swooped low over the cliffside, heading out to sea to confront the dragon. Then he saw her below him, chained to the cliff between the three guard dragons.

He almost turned back to help her, to kill the guards and pull her from the chains. But that wouldn't stop what Bartheleme had planned, which had become abundantly clear. He meant to burn her. Besides, those chains were too thick for him to bite through. It would be up to Fiera to use her magic.

So, he continued his course, straight to the mouth of the dragon.

****

Fiera stared after the flash of feathers that had been Efar, even as her guards launched into the night sky in pursuit. Between them and Bartheleme, they would kill her griffin. She had to do something.

Reaching deep inside her, she searched for any whiff of magic, but found only a tiny spark that would not coax to life, no matter how hard she bit her lip.

In desperation, she reached out with her mind, not bothering to block the dragons this time. The drought wouldn't have affected the creatures of the sea as much as those inland. Her call for help brought a chorus of answers.

There was little the fish could do, but the birds came en masse: sea hawks, gulls, kites, terns, falcons, and osprey. She drove them after the dragons.

Fiera couldn't see the battle except for the flames thrown from the dragons. She knew the birds attacked from above, based on the constant cacophony of voices in her head. Efar, she could only assume, was engaged with Bartheleme.

The fight raged far out to sea, so that the balls of fire were mere dots of light sparking in the darkness. Then suddenly, the fight turned and moved closer, so much so that when the fires lit, she could see the combatants. The three guards were nearly finished; one was already gone and the blood streamed from the eyes of the other two as birds clustered around their heads, pecking away.

An exceptionally long burst of flame came and Fiera saw a host of burning birds fall from near Bartheleme. She also saw that he had Efar clasped tightly in his claws, his teeth snapping for the griffin's neck. For his part, Efar was raking against the dragon's gullet with sharp lion feet and eagle talons, but seemed to have little effect.

It was just a matter of seconds before the dragon prince killed her griffin!

What felt like a lightning bolt of love and fear for Efar jolted through Fiera. The tiny spark of magic within her exploded into an inferno. With a crack, the chains that bound her shattered.

She crouched and placed both hands on the rock beneath her.

****

Efar struggled in the grip of the giant dragon. His claws did little damage to the thick reptilian hide and there was only so far he could squirm to evade the snapping jaws that sought his throat. At least there was one good thing: if Bartheleme tried to burn him, he'd burn himself too.

He barked an awkward griffin chirp as a wry laugh. After all the years of searching, he'd finally found his true mate just in time to die. A heavy, ominous sorrow settled over him.

As the thick feeling increased, the air around him sparked with something unseen. He dodged a score of teeth reaching for his neck even as a shadow darker than the night rose behind the dragon, curving overhead and raining seawater down on them.

Efar didn't understand what it was, but he knew it was magic. Fiera had done something to save him. He also knew he had to get away from Bartheleme...right now.

In a sudden gut-wrenching shift, he changed his top half to human, now much smaller, and slid out of the dragon's clutches. The giant beast roared in frustration and fumbled to recapture his prey. At the same time, Efar used his powerful griffin's legs and pushed off

Bartheleme's gullet as hard as he could, arcing away. As the dragon prince reared up to throw flames, Efar snapped back to griffin and fought to push himself out of range with his damaged wing, watching over his shoulder. The shadow that was above Bartheleme crashed down, with fingers eerily like a hand, in an avalanche of rock and sea grime, taking the royal prince into the sea with it.

Within seconds, the water leveled out as if nothing untoward had happened, as if there weren't a giant dragon crushed beneath its rocks. Waves in ripples were the only reminder and they would be gone soon.

On the ledge ahead of him, Fiera waited with her feet planted wide and her hands on her hips. As he landed, she lifted her head and jutted out her chin as if daring him to reproach her about what she'd done. But, when he lowered and spread his good wing for her to climb on, concern filled her eyes and her face softened. She pointed to his injured wing and the burn that twisted down his side. "You're injured. You won't be able to carry me."

He waited, wing still outstretched.

Slowly, she settled onto his back. As he lifted into the air, trying to correct for the unaccustomed weight with his faulty wing, she said, "You did all that for me. It's my fault you were injured."

She shifted her seat, leaning over his bad side, sending them into a crazy dip as he struggled to get back under control. "I can partly fix these feathers. The quill is living, but the individual plumes aren't. I can grow the ones near the gaps bigger and sturdier to help make up for those that are missing." She placed gentle hands on him.

He felt no electric tingles, no coursing of magic, but his wing strengthened, holding the air beneath it better, and his flight stabilized.

Efar flew on a direct southeast line while the sky lightened into dawn. The ground beneath them stayed dry and barren, tree spikes pointing up toward them, as they passed through the northern corner of the drought, out of the dragon's lands, and into the main region affected by the lack of water.

Eventually, he spied an abandoned farm near the road where they were to meet up with Gwen, Captain, and company. He landed and shifted to human while Fiera looked around. She returned with a moth-eaten blanket and handed it to him. "I couldn't find any clothes."

He smiled. Fiera certainly wasn't the same naïve little girl he'd first met. She hadn't even batted an eye at his nakedness.

She'd saved his life.

As if reading his mind, she said, "I don't regret killing Bartheleme. But it will have started a war."

"That's something to worry about tomorrow. Today, it's just us."

Later, they'd join the rest of the group and travel with them. But right now, there was something else he wanted, something he'd wanted for a long time. He took Fiera's hand and pulled her to him.

Inside, the griffin roared.

The End

Publisher's Note
Please help this author's career by posting an honest review wherever you purchased this book.

About the Author

Wendy is a published author living in New Brunswick, Canada, with her husband, Vince, and two cats named after the Blues Brothers, Jake and Elwood. Her first piece to be printed was a short children's fiction, Jet's Stormy Adventure, serialized in The Illinois Horse Network. She attended University of Iowa, honing her craft in their famed summer workshops and writing programs. Since that time, she has published and co-authored numerous books. Several of her manuscripts and short stories have won international awards and have appeared in multiple venues.